D1714075

# Play with
# my heart
# pay with
# your life

Nadine Frye

## Acknowledgments

First, I want to thank Allah for giving me a gift to share with the world. Islam saved my life, and I pray that His light was always upon my soul.

Next, my husband, Anwar Scott, there is nothing in the world like your love. Thank you for loving a woman who came in pieces, and you glued her back together. I would not trade anything in the world for the nights we share our dreams. You randomly start chopping, the laughter we share, praying with you, fasting with you, watching you raise the boys to be men, and your ability to motivate me into my better self. I will continue to write these books while you spread awareness through your platform @DMVHOODZNDNEWZ. I am proud of who you are becoming as a man.

I have the best family in the world. To every Frye, Taylor, Jones, Buxton, Young, Hampton, and Royal that encouraged me and pushed me, I love you all, and this journey was for you as well as me.

My children are my everything, and two of the greatest gifts Allah could have bestowed upon me. Aaqil and Isa are the funniest, loving, smart, caring, and protective sons in the world. Can't wait to watch them grow into Kings and leading their own families. I want a bunch of grandchildren that I can spoil and send back to your house tipping. It may be many years before I get my dream, but in shaa Allah, I will see it.

To Monica, Tiff, and Desaree, you guys are more than Authors that I've bonded with. You've held me up when I faltered, laughed with me, cried with me, prayed for me, and just motivated me to keep fighting in this industry. I love you all, and I promise this sisterhood shall not be broken, and we are rocking for life.

To every last one of my readers/fans, thank you for allowing me to have a platform that you enjoy. Thank you for letting my creativity keep my books in your hands. There are no limits to my mind, so I hope you are here for its many facets.

To Mesha,

Thank you for always being a friend to me and supporting me when I was a newbie in the game. I appreciate all of the late-night conversations about life and how to navigate this book world. Now you have allowed me to join an amazing team, and it's only one way to go from here, and that's up.

# Chapter 1: Isis

"You think that I want to hear your sob story after you took it upon yourself to steal from me? I play about a lot of things, but my money ain't one of them."

"Queen, how is paying my rent a sob story. I had been trying to tell you that I needed the extra money to pay my back rent." This little bitch, Ta'lya had the nerve to try and make an excuse for double-crossing me.

"Well, that sounds like a personal problem to me. I told you when I put your ass on and gave you the game. My cut is always safe from your spending. I don't care if you use that pussy till it falls out, you better have my money, and you better check it in correct." These bitches always want to play stupid to the rules and bite the hand that fed them.

"Okay, can I go now?"

"Oh, you can go as soon as you work off your debt. It's about to be some long days and nights for you. You will need plenty of throat spray, knee pads, and KY Jelly. Your ass will now work the warehouse, until your debt's cleared with interest."

I snapped my fingers, and two of my goons came forward and snatched her out of her seat. She was kicking, screaming, and making all types of threats as if it would stop them from taking her to her destination. One thing I would never do, and that was to entertain the theatrics of a peasant — especially, one whose pussy and soul belonged to me.

In the game of pimping women, you better believe these crafty hoes would try to tell you anything that you wanted to hear. They would lie on their bald-headed granny to avoid paying you your money. You gave a bitch a safe space and a way to put her natural-born skills to use, and that cunning cunt would still try not to pay the one, who made it all possible. That behavior was unacceptable in my Queendom and punishable any way I saw fit, including taking your life. In this organization, there was only one top bitch, and Isis Superiority Torrance A.K.A Queen, could never be a bottom feeder.

Many people wonder how a woman like myself could ever be a madame, and I would tell them my origin story is boring and cliché. My back was against the wall, and I had mouths to feed. I found a niche and took over. All I had to do was show a woman that there was still power in the

P.U.S.S.Y. Just like the story of any woman who stepped into my position, I wasn't always like this.

Before my business in women, I was married, and a consummate wife. I loved my ex-husband down to his holey socks. Like any other woman; I dealt with his cheating, busting my ass for breakfast, lunch, and dinner, and making me look like a fool in the streets. I took all of his fallacies to become nothing more than a trophy. In the streets, my ex-husband's name rang supreme. He was a drug dealer, who had the streets sewn up. When he stepped on the scene, everybody bowed down to Pierre "Showtime" Lance.

I met him when I was only a young girl with stars in my eyes and no knowledge of life and what made the world go round. In my hood, they labeled me a tenderoni since I stood five-five with skin the color of bronze, wide-set eyes, perfect thirty-six C-cup for breast, and an ass that was as ignant as an idiot in accelerated classes, with the perfect bow-legged walk to match. When we first locked eyes, I felt my whole world spin. I knew that by any means necessary, I would be his all and vice versa.

I should have known that any man that stood six foot four with a body chiseled to perfection and the most fluent chocolate skin with waves in his otherwise curly hair, might come with some type of bullshit. Then that pretty motherfucker had the nerve to have the thickest, longest dick known to man with the stroke to match. All the issues that were dangerous to a young girl, who didn't know the truth of her pussy. So, my love and loyalty were connected to my G-spot, and he worked that shit till I was brainwashed.

I knew that with his status came fans, groupies, and haters. For years, I was just like any woman out here, fighting for the place of "Ride or Die." I loved him, kept his secrets, and when he failed, I forgave him. Any bitch that looked at him for too long got beat the fuck up. If you fucked my nigga--because everybody knew he belonged to me--I would drag a bitch from here to Timbuktu, and that's if I didn't put the bitch in a ditch. It wasn't shit I wouldn't do for that nigga, even if that meant moving his work, or busting my guns beside him. I took his empire and built him a Kingdom.

After three years of me crying late nights, killing niggas and disrespectful bitches, solidifying his position in the streets, and proving my worth; then he decided to marry me. We got married, and for a while, that placated me, but a man would be a man, and my man was just like the rest. The only difference is I had his last name, so I began to feel that no matter what a bitch tried to do or prove, she could never have him as I did. It didn't mean I allowed the disrespect. I still fucked bitches up, who thought it was cool to have any dalliance with my husband, but it didn't bring me out of character too much because I was a wife.

Then I got pregnant and for some reason, that made my husband happy beyond measure. He started coming home at night, eating dinner with me, and the women were no longer a problem. All this man cared about was protecting his legacy and finally having heirs because we found out we were having twins. He bragged to anyone who listened that he was not only having one son but two. Pierre was around here skipping and shit, talking about how he had super nut.

All that came to an end when we found out that those sons were daughters. That knowledge had him switching his style up. Now, he was back in the streets heavy; being disrespectful. Pierre would stay gone for days at a time and acting like the family we had at home didn't matter. He left me to give birth by myself and pretty much raise them alone. Even with that, I still remained loyal. When he found his way home, I fucked him, fed him, and gave him peace of mind.

Then, I started noticing that his clothes were disappearing, and then eventually, he just didn't come back. I'd been in the house stressed with raising two toddlers alone and worrying about a man that left us out there for dead. One day, divorce papers came, and I contested nothing. Unlike most young dummies, I didn't squander away all the fortune he gave me by tricking out on the latest fashions and cars. I was content to leave that big old mansion we lived in and begin over for my daughters. Until the day I was moving out. Pierre pulled up to the house with another woman, and a son in tow.

This funny style, acting nigga, decided to go out and build his dream family with an off-brand bitch. My daughters hadn't seen him in more than a year, and when they ran-up on him to hug him, he acted like my daughters were nothing and pushed them away from him. That was the straw that broke the camel's back. So, after securing my children in the car, I didn't act a fool or show any emotion. All I told him was, *"Today would be a day that you regret, and you will never hear from us again, but you gon' feel me."*

I made that vow, and I didn't rest until I saw him out there hurting. One day, Pierre looked up, and his connect had cut him off, then half his team was gone, and eventually, there was a new sheriff in town. All that knowledge I gained from his pillow talking and being hands-on in his business was his downfall. All it took was a few well-trained pussies, and a few power moves, and this Queen now reigned supreme. He wanted to leave his legacy to his namesake, and I took my daughter's birthright from him.

That was about eighteen years ago, and now I was on to bigger and better things. My daughters, Makeda and Nefertiti, were twenty-one-year-old geniuses, who graduated from college at fifteen and had been the most valuable asset to my team. Speaking of which, I had to get out of there. That damn Makeda was worse than me when it came to their time being wasted. I needed to crunch some numbers with them anyway and see how the expansion was coming along.

## Chapter 2: Makeda

I didn't understand why my mother chose to try my patience as she did, but she was going to learn that my time was valuable. I had a company to run, and if I called for a meeting, then that meant business was at hand, and shit has gotten critical. It was hard tolerating the insolence my mother showed me because she was head of the family.

As I was stewing in my attitude, the front door to my sister and I's house opened and closed. My mother came zooming around the corner like a bat out of hell. At the sight of her, I got pissed again and was about to go in on her, when she put her hand up to stop my predicted rant.

"Listen, little girl. I don't have time to argue with you, today. I know that I'm late, and all that good shit, and you don't have time for tardiness because you are running a business and all that jazz. Now, let's move on since we got all that dumb shit out the way. Where is Nefi?" She said all of that in one breath.

"My twin is upstairs, tinkering away on a computer. Trying to make sure your legacy is secure. I will call her down in a moment. Where are you coming from, and why are you rushing?" I asked about her flustered and slightly disheveled appearance.

"I just had to send one of my girls to work the warehouse for shorting me my money." I knew she was on some bullshit today, and I had no time for her shenanigans.

"Mom, please tell me that this woman shorted you thousands for you to punish her and make her work at the warehouse. Please, let this not be a power trip."

I felt a headache coming on, and I hoped her answer wasn't going to make me kirk out.

"No, she shorted me two hundred-dollars."

This lady either lacked comprehension, or the power she possessed had finally cooked her brain. The warehouse was a brothel for newcomers in our organization. It catered to the everyday joe that was limited on finances but had big fantasies. You could find some of anything going down at the warehouse.

We started most of the ladies there as a test to see how they would respond to a slow grind. Once we saw that they had the motivation to make a dollar out of fifteen cents, we upgraded them to real clientele. That point was why I was perplexed as to why this is the avenue, she chose for such a trivial amount.

"Mom, are you kidding me, right now? Two-hundred dollars is all it took for you to send her to a place we use for our enemies, who steal thousands from us or for the women just starting. The warehouse isn't meant to be used for you to throw petty ass temper tantrums that end in a power trip." I had to remind her crazy ass because she was looking at me as if she was struggling to comprehend.

"So, she didn't steal from us?"

"Mom, two-hundred dollars is equivalent to two cents, especially when put it up against all the money we have in our possession."

"Well, Makeda, I like my change."

I grabbed the bridge of my nose because I felt myself about to blow up. Rigorously, I ran my hand through my kinky twist as I started counting backward from one hundred. It was a tool I used to keep my anger at bay. My mother was the only one that could make me feel like I wanted to destroy the world with her inside. Her logic, most of the time, really fucked with my mind. I loved her crazy ass even though I wanted to commit her *insane in the membrane* acting ass for life.

Hearing footsteps behind me, I turned around and saw my identical twin, Nefertiti. Sometimes staring at her was freaky. We were identical down to the shape of our feet. The only difference we had was her need for glasses because she was practically blind without them. The glasses were the only way people told us apart, and it helped us in our line of work.

When Nefertiti stepped into the room and saw our mother, she ran to her like the little girl she still was on the inside. They began their ritual of rubbing noses and kissing each other's faces. The sight of their corny display of affection was nauseating. Out of the both of us, my twin desired human touch from those whom she loved. I was more stand-offish and solitary but never with my twin. If I needed affection, I got it from Nefertiti only. Shit, we shared a womb, and it doesn't get any closer than that.

"Alright, you two break it up. Let's get this meeting underway and set up a course of action."

"Why the hell are you so hard, Keda?" my mom asked me in a scolding tone, since I broke up their little cuddle party.

"Mom, I was raised by a queen pin, who pimps women for a living. I don't think that necessarily calls for me to be a bunny."

"One of these days, I'm a pop you in your smart mouth. You lucky you are the spitting image of me, and I would never hurt myself." I had to laugh at her reasoning because she proved me right about her being crazy every time.

"I appreciate you for letting me borrow the face that just saved my life. Now, Nefi, please explain to our mother what you found while working on your toys."

"Well, while I was running through general security checks; I kept getting notifications that someone was trying to dig into your information. They were looking deeply, and I decided to ghost their computer, so I could see where the particular inquiry was coming from," my sister meekly explained.

"Who the hell is it, and what do they want?" my mom asked with her impatient ass. My sister pushed her glasses up on her nose before she continued.

"That's the thing. This person has the same level of computer skill as me, if not better. I was only able to ghost his mainframe for about forty-five seconds before his firewalls blocked me and tried to send a virus that would let them do the same for my system. I had to start a self-destruct sequence and pull the drives out of our main system. That is why I was locked away, trying to integrate our info into the back-up system." I could tell that the information that my sister gave had my mom a bit frustrated.

"Nefertiti, what does all of this mean? If someone is looking into me, then that means that the empire is at stake," my mom implored while biting her nails nervously.

"That's why I called you here. I thought that this might be a setback, but it doesn't count us out. Nefertiti is amazing at technology, but I think this particular issue may need a little old-fashioned elbow grease."

"How much elbow grease are we talking?" my mom asked.

"Mom, you might have to come off the porch for this one. This task will need the ultimate amount of finesse. You are going to use your power of persuasion to make the enemy show their hand."

I saw that look of excitement in her eyes and the cogs turning in her head. It had been a while since my mom had been in on the action associated with our empire. That's why they called her the Queen. When my mom got an idea; she played it out until the end. That was the thinking I needed because if she failed, we would all fall, and failure was not an option.

## Chapter 3: Pierre

I looked both ways nervously as I crossed the street, thinking that maybe someone was watching me. It was funny how the same streets I ran, now didn't feel safe for me anymore. The streets out here didn't look the same, and they forgot the one that fed many. It'd been that way ever since I'd lost the chokehold, I had on them. When I used to view the world; it was with everyone at my feet. Nobody could ever tell me there would come a day when Pierre "Showtime" Lance wouldn't be the ruling factor on these Philly streets.

I jumped off the porch at fifteen, and by the age of eighteen, I had the streets sewn up. Man, I had more money than I could ever spend. The bitches flocked to me not just because of my good looks, but because standing in my shadow gave them some status, even if it was minute. You couldn't tell me anything; I walked where I wanted, businesses catered to my needs, bitches threw me pussy like I was a charity case from a third world country, and the streets feared me.

I'd made a name for myself by putting the murder game down anytime, anyplace. That was how I earned the nickname Showtime. Wherever you crossed me, was where I left your brains. It could be in the daylight, in front of the pope or on your mom's lap, it didn't matter to me. Anywhere, anytime could be the place where I departed your soul from your body.

I was good out there in the streets that revered me and living life on my terms with no responsibilities. That was until I turned twenty-three. This young stallion became to object of my affection, and her beauty snatched my attention. I wouldn't lie; I had been checking shorty's fresh. She was thick and bronze and known around the way as a head buster. I dug shorty's confidence and her no-nonsense attitude.

Eventually, we started kicking it, and I promise, Isis was my perfect fit. Although young, Isis matched my attitude and my grind. But like all young rich niggas, I wasn't ready to be tied down to any bitch. Even though I had her attention and loyalty, it was nothing like a new bitch to break in, but Isis didn't make it easy to cheat.

Naw, Isis was a problem, and she caught all the smoke behind me. If she found out a bitch eyeballed me; Isis would swell a bitch's eye sockets. Any bitch I stuck my dick in, ended up somewhere stanking or laid up in the hospital faking amnesia. I got tired of having to pay for funerals and silence. I saw that she was ten toes down for a nigga, so I did what was only right, and that was wife her.

After I gave her my last name, Isis had access to my Kingdom and status; she only dreamt about achieving. I elevated her life like nobody's business. My hard work had Isis sitting in a mansion when she was only used to Section-8 living. Isis had everything a girl could desire, and what did she do? She showed her ingratitude by underhandedly taking everything I worked for my entire life.

Could you imagine how I felt watching a team I built switch sides? We became enemies overnight, and the reasons varied. Of course, we had our issues, and the marriage ran its course after she birthed my daughters. I didn't know I would feel that much grief at the fact that her womb was deficient. How could she give me daughters and expect me to feel like she gave me the world?

All I wanted in life was a few namesakes. After every worldly comfort, I provide Isis, the least she could have done was give me sons to carry on my legacy. At almost thirty with no heirs, and my first try at parenthood; she'd cursed me with daughters, and I felt like she betrayed me. My feelings didn't matter to her, and Isis went against

21

the grain by doing the only thing she knew how, and that was using her pussy to take away my life.

I woke up one morning, and I had no connections, no team, no fans, and nothing to show for my life's blood, sweat, and tears. My downfall was the product of me loving an ungrateful bitch that got too big for her britches. Isis took the game that I taught her and stripped me of my title and dignity. That was why I was standing outside of this person's home. I knew Isis didn't think I, for one second, had forgotten how she destroyed my good name. Nope, revenge was a dish best served cold, and I would be the coldest to ever do it.

I hit the buzzer, and the person I came to see buzzed me up. When I get to the top of the fifth-floor walk-up, there was only one door. Once outside the door, I knocked and waited to gain entrance.

"Hello, Mr. Lance, please step inside." I took his invitation, and it looked like a nerd's paradise.

There were at least five monitors; all running through different types of sequences. I looked up, and there were two sixty-inch screens with split video images. I didn't understand what any of it meant, and it was all rocket science to my thinking. He took a seat at the computer screen and began to pull somethings up to print them off. Using his chair, he slid over to the printer to collect the paperwork. When he slid back over, he handed me a stack of papers about an inch thick.

When I started perusing the packet, the first page had a recent picture of Isis. I would be lying if I said she didn't look just like the tenderoni I married. She had barely aged, and that melanin was popping as the young ones said. I stared, almost transfixed at her image before thumbing through the stack. Page after page were pictures of her in different walks of life.

After the pictures, there was a full docket of her life. It included financial statements and looking at all those zeroes instantly made me angry. This bitch took everything from me and left me nothing. I promise you, I desired nothing more than to see this bitch destroyed.

"I see all this information, and it's good. When can we move on to the next phase of the plan?" I asked him.

"I had already contacted my guy about the plan, and all things are a go. I also wanted to point out that Isis is well-protected. I had a helluva time even digging up that. Whoever they have working on her team erased the information as fast as I could get it.

Her techie even ghosted my computer, and that's not easy to do as I have government level clearances on all of my PCs. I think if there is that type of intelligence around her, this plan may not be so easy." I didn't want to hear shit that little computer geek had to say.

"I know what the fuck I want, and it is that bitch's head on a platter. Just get your guy to do everything that I laid out in front of him, and I can guarantee the bitch will crumble."

I got up and dropped the envelope full of money on his computer table and took my leave. Nothing was going to stand in the way of me and my revenge. What was even sweeter is the fact she would never see this one coming.

## Chapter 4: Isis

I was in the gym on a treadmill, trying to work out some stress. Ever since my daughters dropped that info in my lap, I had been a paranoid patty. I didn't feel like anything was safe, and that put me in survival mode. In the last, almost two decades, I never had to look over my shoulder because no one had ever stood against me and won. If I was honest, it frustrated me that someone dared even to test me.

I ran the last mile on the treadmill, then hopped off and began to cool down. Once I reminded my muscles that it was safe to be normal again, I picked up my towel and headed into the shower. Mindlessly walking, I ran smack dab into what felt like a brick wall, before I felt strong hands wrap around my waist and steady me from what would have been a nasty fall.

Slightly embarrassed, I gazed up into the eyes of my savior, ready to apologize for my mindlessness. The moment my eyes connected with his ultramarine colored ones; my panties automatically became a mess. My brain had stuttered, and the ability to form any verbiage of my native tongue had left me. The rhythm of my heart changed, and I began to feel lightheaded.

Right there in the arms of this stranger, my mind went on a journey in a kaleidoscope. I saw myself doing naughty things to him and for him. I even saw myself swollen with his child and a plethora of other ridiculous shit. Have you ever met a man and wanted to pledge your womb to him? Neither had I until that demon with blue eyes looked me in my face and stole my breath away.

That's why my thoughts were jarring me. I was in my forties, and I wished a nigga would try to put his life juice on one of these ancient eggs. No sir, I had to break whatever magnetic bonding his soul was trying to take mine through. I'd snapped out of his arms like he branded me and issued him the meanest mug I could muster. His whole aura threw me off, and I refused to be smitten against my will.

"You think your ugly, bug-eyed, big-chested ass might not be walking directly in people's line of view. You damn near cracked my forehead with your swole for nothing having ass." The twelve lies spilled off of my tongue effortlessly. I didn't care, and he wouldn't catch me with the witchcraftery.

What I said amused him because he released the manliest, sexy baritone chuckle my ears had ever partaken. Lawd, please excuse the way my bodily fluids were disrespecting the seat of my biker shorts. I never thought a laugh could make my womb leak, and my heart enter into a state of longing.

"Queen, you are way too magnificent to spew such ugliness. I apologize for being the shield that protected your fall. I could never see the earth disrespect such beauty when it should bow to her." Oh, shit, my legs crossed on their own volition.

*Settle down girl; he cannot come with us.* I was having the strongest talk with my womanly parts. When all she wanted to do was wrap around him and live in his back pocket for easy access; that blue-eyed demon had me standing outside of my mind with his lustrous words. Then like a bucket of ice was dumped on my head, I realized he called my name.

"How the hell do you know my name?" I said with the full sassiness of my melanin. His only response was a chuckle.

"Can't say that I have the pleasure of being privy to that information, but if your mother named you Queen, then I must thank her for blessing you with a title most befitting. One, I wouldn't mind paying homage to."

I cutely giggled at his charm. What the hell? I hadn't ever donned this much skinning and grinning since I was a young one in the streets. I didn't know how the moment shifted, but I did something I'd never done.

"A point, I would love to dissect, the name is Isis," I said to the stranger and stretched my hand out for him to shake. He grabbed my hand and rubbed his bearded cheek across the back of it affectionately, before he placed the gentlest of kisses upon my newly flipped palm. He looked me dead in my eyes as he spoke.

"Isis, a name found in ancient Kemet or modern-day Egypt, as it came to be known. People revered her as a goddess, but she was verily a server of her people. Isis played many roles; primarily as wife and mother, mourner, and healer. She was a role model for women, helped cure the sick and prepared bodies for burial. She also had strong links with the kingship and the pharaohs. Oh, how I wish I were Osiris at this moment."

I was astonished because, to date, I had never met a person, let alone a man, that could give me an honest description of my name outside of complimenting its beauty.

"A man who appreciates his roots and studies his culture. I'm most certainly intrigued, Mr…"

"Fabian, Fabian Moore, pleased to meet your acquaintance. Would you like to grab a smoothie from the juice bar and allow me a few more moments to impress you?"

Today, I was feeling generous, so I accepted his invitation.

We went over to the juice bar inside of the gym. We ordered our drinks of choice before we grabbed a table to take a load off. Almost instantaneously, the conversation was sparked. It wasn't long before the drinks were gone and were still running off at the mouth. The conversation flowed so easily as we ran through a range of topics and had in-depth discussions and even an intellectual debate. The moment reminded me of a Jill Scott song since we talked about Moses and Mumia, reparations, and blue colors. It was a Love Rain type of moment.

The Juice Bar attendant interrupted our conversation as she started wiping our table down. When I moved my phone out of the attendant's way, I saw the time and realized we had been talking for hours. Now we sat in companionable silence, smiling at each other as if we were two teenagers, who discovered a love for the first time.

I took a moment to fully take in his presence. It was funny to me that I'd do that last, instead of before he partook in hours of my life. He was not normally my type because he was light-skinned, and I didn't like shit light-skinned but some biscuits. To top it all, he had them funny colored eyes that had been known to get plenty of men's heads split to the white meat.

Fabian's beard was full, and his hair was tapered on the sides with his curls popping in the middle. His lips were full, and his teeth were reminiscent of a Colgate commercial. All the things packaged together would have me out in the world, raising the murder rate. Mama always told me never to date a man prettier than me.

The point could be debated on if his looks could be pretty for a man, but the way he carried himself, you wouldn't dare disrespect him with such an effeminate assessment. Fabian was all man, and for the first time in a long time, I fancied myself smitten. But honestly, I didn't have time to be taken with any man.

Fabian stood and extended his hand to me. I nestled mine in his as he pulled me out of my seat.

Side by side, we left the juice bar and made our way in the direction of the parking lot.

"Where is your car parked?" Fabian asked as we entered the parking lot.

"It's right over there, the chrome on chrome Benz truck," I responded, and the look he gave me was one of appreciation. At least I hoped that was what I saw in his eyes because envy could be disguised behind well-wishing.

We had arrived at my truck, and I hit the key fob to unlock my doors. Fabian reached around me and opened my door, and I climbed inside. Ever the gentleman, Fabian buckled me in before he stepped back and closed my door. I sat there in the front seat in a daze. They said chivalry was dead, but this man embodied all that was male. I must have zoned out because I heard a rapt knock on my window. I shook out of my daze and started the car before rolling my window down.

"You okay, beautiful?"

"Yes, just catching my breath before I left."

"Well, okay. Thank you for the enlightened conversation, and the opportunity to live in your world momentarily. I wanted to know if it was possible to do this again?" Fabian asked me rather eagerly.

"Sure, but my number in your phone, and let's set something up."

Fabian took my number, then waved goodbye before heading in the direction of his car. I pulled out of the parking lot and toward my home. The whole drive I was running through the events of the night. The interactions between Fabian and I were natural as if divinely orchestrated. I'd never felt my soul shake; my mind awakened, nor my body yearning for another to that degree. The realization had me pondering if I had just walked into danger.

## Chapter 5: Fabian

I stood in my kitchen whipping up dinner, trying to put the finishing touches on what would be a delectable evening. It had been a few days since I connected with my target. This job seemed as easy as taking candy from a baby. All it took was a few well-placed looks and some intelligent conversation, and I had her--hook, line, and sinker.

I was what you would call a connoisseur of women. I made my money by making women fall in love with me, and then destroying their lives. It seemed like a cruel task, but all of my victims were heartless bitches, who should have saw it coming. I'd been privileged to know the reality of women, especially black women, who thought themselves important, instead of the bottom feeders they were. If you gave these gutter rats the world, all they would do was try to take everything from you. That's why my services were necessary.

Take my life, for example. I'd met my first and only love in high school. My woman was bad and had everything that a man could desire in a woman. Her body was stacked like kablam-clack-pow, she was soft-spoken, she could cook, still had her virtue intact; all makings of a wife. I married her fresh out of high school, then went straight into the navy to help put us both through college. I served my country and my wife.

I moved up quickly in the ranks, so I decided to make a career out of the navy. I'd purchased my wife a house, gave her access to my money, helped her start her practice, and even gave her children to deal with the loneliness of my absence. Oh no, that wasn't good enough for the ungrateful wench, that I took out of the hood and gave the American dream. No, this bitch wasn't content until she took my soul and dignity.

I'd just came off of my last and longest tour of duty, which ended up being two years. I was overjoyed to be coming home and free from any further duty to the government. I was ready for civilian life and the opportunity to watch my children grow up and become a proper husband for a wife, that exercised patience with my demanding career. Imagine my surprise, when I got to my home, and this cunt was living in my house with some thug, and both my sons were calling him daddy. To add insult to injury, this bitch was a good eight months pregnant.

That scene tore my insides to shreds, and my heart became frostbitten. I beat the shit out of her baby father, almost taking his life. You would think that she felt guilty or at least apologetic. Hell no, this bitch called the cops on me and told them I came home and attacked her husband. Luckily, I had my credentials on me and was able to discredit her lie.

I told the good officers of the law, my story of how I was fresh off a tour of duty. How I had spent the last three years fighting for our country, only to come home and find the hoe with my last name, in my house with her lover. Those lovely boys in blue locked her pregnant ass up and put her side nigga in the ambulance cuffed. It was like at the moment they locked her up; I got a sick sense of gratification at her suffering. That feeling became the addiction I chased until my high was sated.

I called a few buddies of mine, who put me in touch with a lawyer, who filed some emergency injunctions that gave me custody of my two sons with restraining orders, before the sun rose the next morning. Before she walked her ass out of the seventy-two-hour hold, I had the divorce papers drawn up. When it was all said and done, I destroyed her life.

My lawyer painted such a brutal picture of her actions in court, and I was awarded full custody of not just my sons but the daughter she carried in her belly. She had to pay me child support for all three, as well as render me half the earnings from her business. She ended up only being allowed supervised visits with the children for an hour twice a week.

It took three years for her to go bankrupt. Nobody wanted to seek advice from a woman who would dare cheat on a veteran. Her name carried no more weight, and she hit rock bottom. In her misery, I found the definition of true happiness, and I would live my life trying to attain that euphoria continuously.

I heard the doorbell rang, and I turned my pots down low then proceeded to answer the door. I answer the door just as my esteemed guest went to ring the bell again. My guest that stood there with skin bronzed to perfection, was my latest conquest.

"Isis, welcome to my humble abode. You look delectable." She blushed, but I told no lies.

Even in her mid-forties, Isis was a force to be reckoned with. She was a little thicker than slim thick, but not quite a BBW. Her hips enough shake to tip the Richter scales. I took a step back and allowed her entrance into my home. On heeled feet, she walked in my door. When she noticed I had hardwood floors, she bent down to take her shoes off.

Before she could completely bend, I dropped to my knees and grabbed her foot and removed them for her. I allowed my hands to slightly run up her calf teasingly. My touch was soft and barely ghosted her skin, and she was shivering. I stood to my feet and extended my hand for her to take, and I led her to the dining room.

When we reach my table, I pulled her chair out, and once she sat, I scooted her to the table. The table was set up for two, but it seated six. I poured her a glass of red wine that I had chilling before her arrival. Once I was sure her libation was to her liking, I excused myself to the kitchen.

In the kitchen, I stacked her plate with a lemon rosemary rack of lamb, seasoned red potatoes, and asparagus. I put fresh rolls on her plate, then took it into the dining room and made a flair of presenting Isis her meal, and her eyes lit up.

"This looks delectable. I can't wait to dig in," she said as I headed to the opposite end of the table.

I tucked my napkin in my shirt before I picked up my glass of wine and admired Isis as she ate. She dug in with gusto, and the way she was moaning, indicated her meal was satisfactory. I'm glad I used an old family recipe to get the lamb to fall off the bone. Isis grabbed her napkin and wiped her mouth.

"Oh my God, Fabian, this is so scrumptious. Here I am just stuffing my mouth. Where is your food?" she asked when she noticed that my plate was empty.

"Mine is preparing. The last time we talked, you told me you were a single mother. Would you care to share how someone as intelligent as you found themselves raising her queens alone?"

"Well, sometimes, you find yourself in a situation where you have no choice. In an ideal world, one would dream of having their family be a cohesive unit. Becoming a single mother was not a part of the plan, but it was a role that I've adapted to and excelled in. What doesn't kill you will make you stronger."

"You have twins, and I know that it is not an easy task. Tell me about them."

"My daughters are everything to me. There is not a more fulfilling role in life than being their mother. They have exceeded all my expectations and given me the best memories of my life. They are intelligent, entrepreneurs, and testaments to everything I've ever done right in life."

"How has their father's absence in their life affected the way you parented them?"

"His absence, although unfortunate, didn't change anything. I was up to the task, and I did it proudly from the muscle." Isis' answers to my questions almost caused me to show my disgust outwardly, but I was too thorough at this game.

Her answers, although evasive, let me know everything I read in the file on her had to be true. She was independent and vengeful. Isis took this man's kids and acted like it was normal. I got the answer to Ms. Independent's sneakiness.

"Are you ready to bring my meal to me?" Her brows knitted in consternation at my question, before she answered me frantically.

"I'm sorry, Fabian, was I supposed to bring something and forgot," I chuckled sexily at Isis' response.

"You remembered; I assure you. Now drop your dress and come put that pussy in my face. I'm starving."

Just like that, her eyes glazed over as she stood hurriedly to follow my command. I spent the evening into the wee hours of the morning, solidifying my position. I put this dick in her life and in any hole I chose. When I finished loving her down, she was weeping and ready to pledge her life to me. Phase one of this mission was complete, and now it was time for the takeover.

# Chapter 6: Nefertiti

I'd felt the panic starting to rise in my chest as soon as I left the house. I was in my car trying to be brave in a big world that felt all-consuming. It didn't seem like an accomplishment compared to those that littered it daily, but for a germaphobe like me, being in public was conquering Mount Olympus. As common as it was to spread germs through human contact, you would think that people would be more wary of the outside world, instead of frolicking around this cesspool of death.

I was on the hunt for pieces that I needed for a tablet that I was building for my sister. I planned to turn the tablets into advanced walkie-talkies. There was only one place in Philly that I patronized for parts, and that was NTR or Nonprofit Technology Resources. The organization served low-income families in Philadelphia by recycling used computers, providing hands-on training, and assisting community-based service organizations to use computers effectively in their work.

I used to volunteer at NTR when I was in high school, and I came there to spend my money on parts and sometimes donate systems that they could utilize in their classroom settings. It was my way of helping give back to my community.

I parked my car, got out, and hurried inside. When I stepped into the warehouse, I saw that there was a class in progress. I'd stopped to listen in, and I was impressed with the subject matter. The instructor was explaining to them the difference between the clock cycles of a computer versus a tablet. He was patient in engaging them in the debate concerning how the tablet ran slower, but the clock cycles are underpowered to conserve battery life and operate for quick basic commands. The students were getting animated with their responses, and it was a subject I'd enjoyed on an elemental level. Watching them reminded me why technology made sense, and it was my career of choice.

"Excuse me, welcome to NTR, how may I assist you?" the receptionist's voice rudely broke my reverie.

Her voice carried across the counter in a premier ethnic fashion. I hated to use the word ghetto when describing my fellow black people. The receptionist's voice carried so far that the instructor turned to the area to see what was happening up front. Why would he go and do that? Even with glasses on, the instructor's eyes had drawn me into their depths. I was not the typical female that went goo-goo gah-gah over beings of the opposite sex. Men weren't my concern as I'd focused on attaining excellence through education. To date, I'd never been in a relationship, nor had I ever taken a second glance at any male. Until I locked gazes with that man, and he had my rapt attention.

He had to be perusing me just as introspectively as I'd done him because we stood there in an intense stare down. I decided to be hospitable and wave at him to break up the awkwardness of our transfixed gazing. He shocked me when his light skin inflamed red, and he turned away shyly. That reaction had me more than a little intrigued because shyness wasn't generally attributed to men, but it looked good on him. With his attention back on his class, I could return to the matter at hand and address the receptionist.

"If you minded lowering your tone, I would be more than a little gracious to have your assistance," I told the receptionist sternly. The receptionist blanched from the steel in the tone I used but moved to make the proper corrections to her manners.

"I apologize. My voice is just naturally loud. What can I do for you, today?"

"I'm looking for pieces to build a tablet,"

"Okay, hold on, I will get the tech specialist that deals with parts. *Fahrice!* Your assistance is needed upfront."

That incorrigible human had yelled clear across the warehouse with no couth or concern for her voice disrupting an active class. The instructor had turned toward her and outwardly cringed at being summoned unprofessionally. I grabbed the bridge of my nose and pushed my glasses up. The receptionist was well on her way to grating on my last nerve. Her conduct dictated that I could no longer be nice.

"First of all, this is a business. It would have taken you seconds to walk over to the instructor; two seconds to tap him, five seconds to tell him that he was needed, and seven seconds to walk back. Twenty seconds out of your life is all that it would have taken for you to be the consummate professional.

"Instead, you chose to use deplorable manners and unsatisfactory practices to become remedial in your job. I would suggest that you get an employee handbook and sit down and familiarize yourself with the proper protocols of this company and what's required of its employees.

"While you're at it, please get to HR and ask for a proper description of your job title to aide you in being more effective in your position. Furthermore, stop rolling your eyes at me before I help them to become stuck permanently."

The receptionist stomped off from her post in anger. All you could hear was her mumbling and then copious amounts huffing and puffing. I wondered whose house she was going to blow down with all that big bad wolf posturing she was doing. The little worker bee was about to meet the quiet storm if she didn't calm down. In my mind, I was planning ways to stop her heart for making me check her, when my musings were interrupted.

"Excuse me, did you need my assistance?" a voice as deep and as smooth as velvet asked me, and my head whipped around.

The instructor, Fahrice, as the receptionist called him, was in my personal bubble. With him being that close to me, the first thing I'd noticed was the vivacity in his eye color. Fahrice's eyes were a cerulean-hazel blend and offered you a look into what could only be a marvel of God. With him in my personal space, I'd started feeling parched. Maybe I should have went and checked my blood sugar. That wouldn't have been right since I'd eaten before I got there. I cleared my throat before I responded.

"Yes, I'm looking to purchase parts for a tablet." He pushed his glasses up on his nose before he responded to my inquiry.

"What seems to be wrong with your device? Maybe I can help?"

He responded like a typical male human that saw a woman in a store. We become the proverbial damsels in distress in search of a man to fix our problems.

"There is nothing wrong with my device. I'm looking for the parts to aide me in building one."

When I said that, he looked at me with sincere admiration, and that caused me to blush deeply. With his eyes alight, he led me through the warehouse into the section that housed all if the technical parts.

"Back here, you will find everything you need to build a tablet, whether they are suited for android or iOS. Here in these sections, you'll find accelerometers, gyroscopes, graphics processors flash-based memory, Wi-Fi and cellular chips and antennas, USB docks and power supply speakers, touch-screen controller chips and camera sensors, chips and lenses. The basics for all your building needs," he said with all the giddiness of a true computer geek.

We walked together, inspecting different parts as he expounded on their different uses as if I was clueless, but it was nice to talk to someone who understood my language. As I perused his selection, I was thoroughly impressed. Every piece was stacked neatly in its place and shining like a beacon for inquiring eyes.

It felt like I was traversing through a real-life cyber world. What tripped me out was, all of the parts were top of the line and not typically found in the little back yard shop of a non-profit. The parts I saw could rival anything currently sold on the black market. That made me look at him a little more closely.

I began grabbing everything that I needed for my project. Every time I choose something, he would nod in approval. That gave me a funny feeling in my tummy. *Oh God, please don't let me have gas. If so, at least let it wait until I got to the car. Let not my body do strange things in front of this perfect stranger* was the mantra on repeat in my mind.

"Would you happen to have any antennas that can be attached to the tablets. I'm playing

Comment [KF]: It is recommended inner thoughts are italicized to disting it from normal text.

Comment [nF]: Thank you for that information

Comment [nF]:

around with an idea for radiolike activity." I asked him, and his eyes became crazed.

"What would you need with something as anachronistic as outside antennas?"

Fahrice's question sounded sarcastic like he was calling me an idiot nicely. That pissed me off severely

"Let me tell you something, Mr. 'Ask what has already explained'. Since you ride the little-wittle buses on Saturdays, I will tell you again. I want to give my tablets radiolike activity or in layman's terms turn them into walkie talkies. Something someone with your knowledge should have been able to figure out. Talking to me like I'm some foreign type of idiot."

Fahrice bit his lip and smiled as if my attitude amused him. Then he boldly walked into my space and lifted his glasses from his eyes and placed them on his head. Those eyes were right there in 3-D, and lawd have mercy, I felt my heart palpitate. It felt like I was about to have a heart attack. *Please God, don't choose today to be the day that I fell out from unattended medical issues, I didn't even know I had.* My heartbeat was erratic and felt like it was ready to burst. It was that moment when I thought it was all over; he chose to speak again.

"Lovely, I would never question your intelligence. From our brief interaction, I know that you are anything but a dolt. My question was supposed to be the reason you asked me, where you were going wrong, and I would have told you. Since you have trouble following the signal, I gave you in my Socratic question, I will ask you outright.

"Why would you use outside antennas when everything in life is now wireless? It would be easier to build an app that can give you the functionality you seek. I would have then offered to help you if you didn't know how. Now, will you be willing to allow me to assist you with this project, or are you going to continue telling me what I don't know."

Well, shyness be damned. It was like Fahrice transformed into an alien right before my eyes. He was no longer the awkward and unassuming man I believed him to be. Oh no, I saw him, and it was a sight to see. The tone of his voice had me checking to see if my baby hairs laid properly and if my outfit was pressed. I didn't know where the sudden burst of ticks in my limbs came from, but I wasn't particularly fond of the feeling. I answered him the way my heart delegated my speech to answer.

"Sure, that would be much appreciated," I said, quieter than I had before when I'd thought I was handing him his ass.

"Well, consider it a date."

We exchanged information, and I headed back out through the warehouse. At the front, I made my purchases, and then left out and headed to my car. The whole drive to my house, I was confused. I needed someone to make me understand exactly what just transpired in the store. Well, I would be waiting for my twin to get back because I felt like something just happened that went over my head.

## Chapter 7: Makeda

Tired didn't even begin to describe the weariness in my bones. I had been away from home on an assignment for my twin and I's company, Measure for Measure. Our company was the place where wives came to get their just due from men; who chose to play with their hearts, in their faces, and all over their lives. We prided ourselves on being the place that women get recompense for their time, love, and tears. All things that undeserving men took for granted, until we made them see our hearts weren't a game.

People often wondered why two college graduates, who graduated top of their class at fifteen, with a 4.8-grade point average and an IQ of 177 and 175 respectively, would choose to go into our line of work. Well, the answer was simple: we were our mother's children. Although anyone who met our mother, Isis, automatically saw her as tough and insufferable; everything had a reason. They would never understand the woman she was before her heart turned cold.

Back then, my mom was always smiling and singing. My earliest memory with her was around two years old. Our mom would sit and read the dictionary to us and plan activities to help us understand the word. No matter what we were doing; she always read to us, even if she was cooking, cleaning, or bathing us. Her eyes would be so bright, and the lilt in her voice was so soothing and held our attention easily. We were her points of pride and joy, and you could tell by how she nurtured us effortlessly.

All of that changed when we were three. I know it might seem a little young to remember, but my twin and I did. At three, we could read on a third-grade level, do math up to our multiplications, and hold conversations to rival any adults. I remember one day, my mom was packing up boxes. We didn't understand why, but my mom made it seem like we were headed on an adventure, and that made us excited.

We were leaving, and our father showed up, and it made me happy to see him. I remembered him only by the nights he would come to stay and sleep in the room with my mom. Those mornings after he showed up; she would be really happy. On that day, we saw him outside, and he was with a woman and child. It struck me as an oddity, but I wasn't old enough for details. I was only old enough to understand that I didn't like the scene presented. My sister, trusting as she was, ran up to him and tried to show him love, and he pushed her as if she was a disgusting peon.

That day, what I felt for him, died. My sister had always had soft feelings, so you could imagine how distraught she was to have her affections rejected. That day, I saw something enter my mom's eyes, which I now knew as revenge mixed with determination. It wasn't until we were older that my mom sat us down and explained the whole situation to us. She never lied to us and always gave us the truth, raw and uncut.

After listening to her story at sixteen, I vowed that no woman should ever be treated in that manner. Not without getting their piece of the pie for all of their pain and suffering. Oh, you thought my mom didn't tell us how she took our sperm donor for everything he had? Hell yeah, she did, and we are willing to help as many women as we could, get the same. With my master's in Forensic Science with a focus on Investigations and Nefertiti's Doctorate in Computer Sciences with focuses on Computer Forensics and Applied Technology, our company has the holy grail of a team.

I did most of the fieldwork because Nefertiti had no time for germs or the people that carried them; what she brought to the company was invaluable. Nefertiti was the hacker's hacker. If it was in the digital world, she could discover it. She had also patented our computer security systems and made the simplified version of it available to the public. What information she dug up on a mark, I used my superb critical thinking skills to create a plan of action. I also ensured that whatever route we took, all of our bases were covered.

I'd finally pulled up to my crib, and I saw my mother's car in our driveway. I feel an instant headache coming along. I'd go in there and face the music. I opened the front door and went to the living room. Once there, I saw that my twin was in a panic. Nefertiti was sitting Indian style on the couch, rocking her legs and picking the corner of her lip.

The whole time, my mother was there trying to get Nefertiti to tell her what was wrong. Before I could fully step into the room, Nefertiti's head snapped my way. She must have smelled me. When I locked eyes on her, her eyes began to water. I dropped my bag and took off towards her. Slightly, I nudged my mother out of the way, and I dropped to my knees in front of my twin.

Nefertiti appeared so distressed, and I could feel my heart squeezing. Then I had a feeling of anxiety, and I knew that it was coming from her. Being twins; I could feel her straight through our bond, so I placed my hands on her shoulders and laid my cheek next to hers and started rubbing it along hers in an affectionate manner. We had done this to calm each other down since we were really small.

With each rub of my cheek against hers, I felt her begin to relax. Once I was certain she calmed, I pulled back to stare into her eyes. I saw her slowly coming back to me, and I finally breathed a sigh of relief. That was when I heard my mom suck her teeth.

"You same- faced heifers get on my nerves. Here I am, the one that carried you both for eight months, endured a seventy-seven-hour of labor, then received one hundred and thirty stitches because you all decided to come out holding hands, and then raised you all as a single mother. None of my hard labor was enough to console my child. No, she wants to sit here like a deaf-mute and rock until she sees her mirror image. Ungrateful, the lot of you." My mom was big mad when she started using old British women's sayings to describe her feelings.

"Mom, I apologize if you feel overlooked, but can you please let me tend to my twin, and then we will get back to you?" I asked her imploringly, so she could remember that this moment wasn't about her.

"Tuh, I accept that piece of shit sorry, now carry on."

My mom huffed and then slammed back into my sofa. Her behavior was anything but insouciant. A point that made Nefi giggle, and I was just happy to have her back to reality.

"Mommy, don't be like that. You know it's a twin thing. I love you, though," Nefi told her, and that seemed to take some of the steam out of her attitude.

"What made you shut down, Nefi?" I asked her

"Well, for the last few days, I've been trying to figure out if I'm dying. Some strange things happened to me at the computer store on Saturday." I twisted my face up. What was Nefi talking about, dying?

"Why would you think you were dying? Explain to me what happened to give you that impression."

"Well, I left the house, and I felt perfectly fine. Then I went inside and had to lay the cashier out, but that's a story for another time. I was talking to the attendant, when all of a sudden, I felt parched and lightheaded, then my heart started beating fast and felt ready to explode. Then my stomach felt weird, and I thought it was gas. After thinking about the actual feeling, it felt more like how your tummy drops on a rollercoaster. I was so scared and nothing that I can think of made sense."

As I listened to Nefi, I'd mentally started going through my Rolodex of diseases. Nothing that she said went together, but separately, they could be anything.

I felt my anxiety spike, and my fear became gripping. I couldn't lose my twin, and I needed to figure out this mystery. While I was wracking my brain over life-threatening issues, my mom's deep guttural laugh reached my ears. My head whipped in her direction, and she was falling out, laughing all over the couch. Why my twins impending doom was a point of hilarity for her, I didn't know. All I knew was, her childish behavior started pissing me off, and she was making my sister uncomfortable.

"Would you like to tell us what is funny? My sister thinks she is dying, and you are getting your fifty chuckles at her expense," I asked my mom's rude behind self. She sat up and activated her resting bitch face. I knew then that she was about to get in her feelings.

"Listen, little girl. I keep telling you that you gon' get popped in your mouth one of these days.

You always jump o the defense of the child you didn't birth. Now you two geniuses are sitting there with a combined IQ of 352, and you still don't have any common sense. That girl is not about to die, but her life will never be the same."

"You always make things personal. Nefi is your daughter, yes, but we have been bonding since conception. I'm sorry that it makes you feel some way, but it is what it is. If she is not dying and you know everything, how do you explain her symptoms?"

Her smart remarks had me yelling, and that made my mom sit on the edge of her seat. She looked ready to finally make good on her threat to pop me in the mouth. I gulped audibly because today might have been the day that I went too far. She turned to my sister and started firing off questions.

"Was the attendant male or female?"

"It was a male."

"When you got dry-mouthed and lightheaded, what were you doing?"

"He was staring me in my eyes, and all I could think was they were the best God had ever bestowed on anyone."

"When you felt that sinking feeling in your stomach, what was happening?"

"I was looking at different gadgets and picking the best for my project. The more I chose, the more he approved of my choices. It was like it felt good to make him proud."

"When you felt like your heart was beating out of your chest, what was happening then?"

"We were in a little heated debate. But then he walked up on me, and it was like the world stopped. I felt a little anxious but with excitement and not worry. Why are you asking me all these questions? It still doesn't explain why I'm going to die," Nefertiti said frustratingly, and I was having the same trouble as she was; trying to figure out what it all meant. My mom shook her head in disbelief.

"This lets me know that I have done you both a great disservice. Have I been that bitter that the day has finally arrived, and my daughter doesn't even recognize that she is smitten with a man?" Now, it was my turn to look confused.

"Mommy, what do you mean?" Nefertiti asked.

"Baby, all of those things that you felt were a woman's natural inclination to the opposite sex.

When you meet a man that awakens your senses, you feel all the things you felt, just not by those descriptions. You will feel like the earth just left from underneath your feet. Their aura will change the rhythm of your heart just from standing in their presence, and that will cause the butterflies to run rampant. All of these things you felt, but you are so oblivious to the opposite sex, and you would not know the signs.

"Neither one of you has ever been in love, nor knows the beauty of love when it is first sparked. I feel like I sheltered you two and that because of my life, you guys have taken no interest in the very thing that makes life go around. Every love story is not a horror story. Love, when cultivated and nurtured, can grow to be the single most valuable asset one can attain," my mom told her,

My sister broke down crying. My mom rushed over to her and tried to console her as I stood there, in total disbelief.

"Mommy, I don't want to love anybody other than you and my twin. Please, don't make me. Love almost destroyed you, and I don't want that." My sister was inconsolable and reverting to childlike behavior.

"Love is not so scary, and it's just something that you don't understand. The thing about love is that it can be measured. It has levels, and no love is the same. The type of love I had for your father was the dangerous all-consuming, all-needing, blindly trusting in it to give you all you need to live kind of love. It's the love to which many lessons are gleaned, and your mistake table and warning system become activated. It is also the type of love that shows you exactly what love is not.

"It also opens you up to the type of love that builds empires. From every mistake, every tear, every insecure moment, every wringing soul wail that is born from that incongruent love; you will find you will become reborn and able to recognize real love in all its purity. Love should be fluent, patient, motivating, a foundation, given and accepted. Love will grow you and become something that evolves with you as long as it is watered. So never be afraid of love because you were bore from it and born to give it."

I took a moment to ponder my mom's statement. There was more than a little truth to be garnered from the validity of her words. It was crazy that neither one of us ever factored love into the equation of what my sister felt.

When my mom shared her pain with us, Nefertiti and I did take it more than a little bit personal. The aftermath of how my father broke our mother down, was the whole basis of our company. Inadvertently, her misfortune closed us both off to an emotion we deemed moot. Now, she was imploring us to be open to an emotion we never felt was safe. I didn't know what Nefertiti was going to do with this new-found information. For me; it would always be fuck love, and the niggas it was connected to.

## Chapter 8: Fabian

It's been about a month or so since I started this game with Isis. She was by far the easiest target I'd ever had the pleasure of taking for a spin. This woman would come to my house to cook, clean, and cater to my whims. Wherever I got hard is where she would bend over and allow me to empty my balls. I got the good morning texts; Isis didn't make moves without my knowledge and her submission had me feeling kingly. The devotion she offered me would probably move me if I didn't know the type of woman she truly was on the inside.

Her self-importance showed in the lavish gifts she always bestowed upon me as if I couldn't afford to do nice things for myself. It was in how she turned her nose up at simplistic dates to franchise restaurants, overspending money frivolously for expensive dining. Like now; we were on a trip, and when we got to the airport, Isis almost died when she found out we were flying commercial and in coach, none the less. Isis' eyes bulged out of her head, and I thought for a second that she would faint. The moment was more than laughable. If she had been a woman that tickled my fancy, I would have pulled out all the stops. I was a rich man many times over. No, my methods were used to humble her and her sense of entitlement.

I wanted her to remember that she was only worth gold to herself. A bitch like her should always be reminded of their humble beginnings. So, I used the love she gave me so freely, the dick I had in abundance, and the love she imagined in my eyes, to keep her complacent with the little I did offer her.

"Ladies and gentlemen, welcome to Las Vegas McCarran International Airport. Local time is 5:15 pm, and the temperature is sixty-two degrees. For your safety and comfort, please remain seated with your seat belt fastened until the Captain turns off the Fasten Seat Belt sign. This will indicate that we have parked at the gate and that it is safe for you to move about. At this time, you may use your cellular phones if you wish.

Please, check around your seat for any personal belongings you may have brought on board with you, and please use caution when opening the overhead bins, as heavy articles may have shifted around during the flight. Thank you for flying with American Airlines," the flight attendant announced through the overhead system.

I shook Isis awake, and she jumped up as if she was ready for war. Even with her hair slightly tousled, she was absolutely beautiful. I chuckled at her because she acted like more of a soldier than me. Isis always woke up alert and ready, like she was never resting. I had to laugh at that thought.

"Welcome back to the land of the living, sleepyhead. We just arrived at our destination."

"Hey babe, I can't believe I slept the whole flight. It was comfortable in these seats. Who would have known?" Isis facetiously said to me, and it took everything in me not to lay her wanna be bourgeois ass out.

"I would know because no matter where I am in life, I will never be too good to save money." I left Isis standing there with shock at my dig and made my way off the plane.

I had to get the fuck away from her. All I could envision was me snapping her neck. It was like Isis was always trying to make the world believe that she was just this well-rounded and cultured boss. Isis had a way of making it seem like the world was beneath her feet, and I refused to be the peasant underneath her boot.

Before I knew it, I was in front of the console and snatching our bags from the baggage claim carousel. With our bags in hand, I started the trek for the exit. All the while, I could feel Isis sulking behind me, but I refused to turn around and acknowledge her ungrateful ass. Once we made it outside, I pulled my phone out to order an Uber. Luckily for me, it was only one minute away.

When the driver pulled up, I slammed our bags inside the driver's trunk, and we took the five-minute ride over to the Luxor Hotel and Casino. The ride was silent, and that was how I preferred it for right now because one more word out of her, and the mask would have come off. Back at the airport, I almost said fuck this job.

Lately, I'd started to get that urge to kill her and be done with the whole situation. If the payout weren't so large, I would do just that. The Uber pulled up to the front of the hotel in no time at all. We get out, and now, I saw that Isis was looking as sad as an orphaned puppy. She could save that childish shit for a nigga that really cared for her because those goofy eyes weren't moving me.

We check-in, and I grabbed our room keys and headed to the elevator. On the elevator, her leg was shaking, and her eyes were full of tears. Oh well, any hoe that breathed my air was going to have a little more humility, or I would go the extra mile to make them bow down. We arrived on our floor and headed into our room, which happened to be the Tower Elite King room. When we got in the suite, she had the nerve to look surprised. That's what her judgmental ass got for making it seem like she was the only one who could vacation in luxury.

I dropped our bags and went over to the bar and poured me a glass of Hennessey. After a couple of shots, I felt the liquor start to loosen me up. I began to undo my tie, and I took my blazer off. With another glass of Henny in my hand, I went and took a seat in the sitting room of the suite and laid my head back against the sofa. Although fake, this trip was supposed to be a point of relaxation. I wasn't supposed to be in my feelings like this because an ungrateful cunt wanted to kill my vibe.

Nothing about Isis should have affected my world to this degree. I had to get my head all the way together before this plan fell apart. All I had to do was remember the millions I'd receive as a reward for suffering through this sham. I felt a hesitant tap on my leg. My eyes popped open, and I sat up and saw Isis stood before me. Nervously, she was bouncing from one foot to the other as if she was gathering the courage to say what was on her mind. I'd only stared at her intensely, and she took my silence as an invitation to unburden herself.

"I'm trying to figure out what I've done to upset you. You stormed off the plane and basically left me to shadow you as if I were a lost puppy. Then you refused to speak to me, and I don't understand it all."

At her statement, my eyes became steely. It was time to give her a little glimpse of my true nature since she wanted to stand there and villainize me and victimize herself.

"Just like always, you pretend to be oblivious to an issue happening in front of you. It's like you are so above everyday understanding that you just blatantly refuse to use your common sense. Well, if that's the type of ignorance you wanna live in, then I will leave you to your own stupidity."

My tone was abrasive, and it made Isis physically flinch. Then she did something I didn't expect and erupted into tears. It made me look around in puzzlement because I knew, the big bad Isis, wasn't in my face showing emotions. Her tears didn't move me in the least.

"Why are you talking to me like this? I don't even know what I've done to make you say the things you are saying to me."

"You just don't get it, and maybe you never will."

I jumped up out of my seat and prepared to walk around her miserable ass. Before I could get past her, she threw her arms around me to waylay my departure.

"Fabian, please!!! Just tell me what I did wrong. Let me fix it, don't just walk away without letting me correct my actions." I would have felt that in my soul, only if I had one. Now, I was about to capitalize on her show of weakness.

"Isis, your behavior and attitude concerning material possessions disgust me. You turn your nose up at restaurants that aren't five star, and you always want to stay at your house because, as you say, it has more space and the bigger bathroom. You almost died a thousand deaths when you found out we were flying coach.

"I planned this special weekend for us, and you've made it seem like what I've done is not enough. I may not be a millionaire like you, but I do well for myself. I may not be able to take private jets and do the shit you are accustomed to, but, as a man, I try to give you the best of myself. Everything I do is from the heart. Your attitude makes me feel inadequate, and it stalls my efforts. And to think I brought you here to ask you…never mind. Let me go take a walk," I said in a heartfelt manner as I made a show of trying to leave. Who knew that my acting skills had finally reached the Oscar level? I'd almost forgiven myself.

"Fabian, no, please stay here and talk to me," Isis said while latching onto my waist from behind.

"Babe, let me go. I can't sit in here and allow you to shit on my efforts. It's been hard to watch the disappointment in your eyes. I don't know where to begin to make you happy. I don't know how to be enough." I tried to move out of her grasp, but she held me tighter.

"How could you ever think you are not enough? I tell you as well as show you. I'm not that pretentious woman, as you've described. I know what it's like to come up from nothing. I wasn't raised with a silver spoon in my mouth. I am from the slums of North Philly and know firsthand about the struggle. I'm grateful for everything that you do, and I'm sorry if I appear unappreciative of anything that you do.

"You have impressed me, kept me thinking, and you are all that I see. I never what to see myself as anything but the woman who loves you, thanks God for you, values you, and sees you for who you are. Whatever I need to do to fix this, you let me know, and it is done." I spun in her arms and pull her close. Isis had just given me the opening that I'd needed

"Marry me! If all you said is true, then let's start our life on equal footing. You do something for my soul that I've never felt. All the time I have left in this world, I want to spend it as your husband. I see forever in your eyes, and I want to honor the fact that you are my rib. Do you love me enough to merge our lives? Am I worthy of changing your last name?"

"But what about our families? Is this really what you want?"

"Isis, I have wanted nothing more in my life. I don't care about anyone else, at this moment. My heart wants to be entangled in yours until we are old, gray, and beyond."

I pulled the ring out of my pocket, and she started crying harder. I could also see a slight hesitation in her eyes before she nodded her head subtly, then nodding more vigorously.

"Yes, Fabian, of course, I will marry you."

I kissed her as if I were trying to steal her breath away. In a sense, this was synonymous with a kiss of death. Phase two of my plan had been activated, and she didn't even understand the whirlwind that I was about to take her on.

We got married in a chapel in Vegas. I spent about a week with her, solidifying her decision. Now, it was time to get home, so that I could get this show on the road. I was coming to take over her world as a thief in the night.

## Chapter 9: Nefertiti

It'd been a few weeks since my breakdown in the living room. The knowledge that my mom dropped on me concerning love, had left me trying to figure out what to do with this new information. For so long, I just assumed that love was a worthless emotion that could lead you to sleepless nights and revenge. That's why I avoided the opposite sex like the plague. I'd refused to lose weight, sleep, or my sanity over a four-letter word.

I mean, I only watched my mother put on a strong armor and jump headfirst into raising us alone. She cared for us with all of the love in her body, only because my father threw the love that she gave him right back in her face. My mom tried to pretend that it didn't hurt her, but children caught onto more than parents thought even when they tried to hide it from them. I could remember the nights, where my mom thought she cried silently. My little body laid next to her in bed as her shoulders shook, and her body was wracked with sobs.

Holidays had always started late, and I knew she would cry before she started her day. She buried her pain inside of raising us to be conscious, more than a fat ass to a man, and that education was our top priority. Being a mother had never been an area she lacked. My mom was even more astute at business.

Although she started out pimping women and selling drugs, her empire had become even vaster over the years. That is a testament to all of the hard work and dedication she lent to anything that she did. Her motivation was more than just money. She wanted to impact the world.

What woman you know owned produce stores in urban neighborhoods just so little black boys and girls could have access to fresh fruits and vegetables. My mom had restaurants that she turned into soup kitchens on Saturday and Sunday, so the homeless could have free meals in a classy environment. Her domestic violence network helped women and men, providing them with more than a place to stay and giving them the resources to reclaim their life. She built two schools that catered to the arts, and that same school offered scholarships for the less fortunate.

Watching how my mom worked to leave her imprint on the world was the motivation behind all I did in life. She showed me no matter where you began, once you reach your dreams, you should, in turn, become a servant to your people. It was the reason why my sister and I gave back wherever we were needed. My mom led by example and to the world, she was a cold-hearted bitch, but anyone who knew Isis, knew that she overextended herself. I could only hope to become half the woman she was.

That's why when she talked about giving love a chance, I took her advice to heart. To hear such passion in her voice, about a subject she normally avoided, had me doing something I'd never thought I would. At that moment, I decided to reach out to Fahrice. It was the best decision I'd ever made.

It was awkward at first, but Fahrice went out of his way to make me feel secure and comfortable with our newfound arrangement, which was funny because Fahrice was even more awkward than me with social interactions. We, to date, have only talked over the phone and through text. He was witty, a gentleman, and the ultimate gaming partner. I found that talking to him over the phone and through text was way easier than when we were face-to-face. Tonight, we decided that after weeks of connecting over devices, we were going to try a formal date. That was why I was pacing the floors in my room and having an anxiety attack.

I had half of my closet on my bed. I didn't know what to wear or what the social norms were for first dates. I asked Siri, and she only told me to try my best and hope for the rest. The useless device; it only served to exacerbate my feelings of trepidation further. I'd sat down and placed my head upon my knees, trying to calm down and remove all the variables until I solved the problem.

"Sissy, why are you in here wearing the hardwood down, and why does it look like your closet threw up all over your bed?" My head snapped up at my sister's voice. Her presence had an immediate calming effect.

"I don't know what to wear on this date. I think I'm going to cancel and suggest that we do this over Facetime."

"Awwww, come on, twin. You can do this. You've been around here everyday, kee-keeing on the phone on some boo love shit, so why not enjoy the experience of your first date. Where are you guys going anyway?"

"I don't know. All Fahrice told me was to dress comfortably."

"That's easy, sis, you are dressed comfortably all the time. How about you wear your hand-painted and bejeweled washed pink sweatshirt by Visual 3y3. The one that says, "Feed Me & Tell me I'm Pretty." You can match that with any pair of blue distressed skinny jeans, and I would top the outfit off with your gold Christian Louboutin Lou spikes Woman Lame sneaker shoes.

"Un-twist your Bantu knots and let your curls hang out. I got the perfect headband for you. Now, run along and get dressed while I put all of these clothes back in your closet. This mess is making me itch."

One thing for certain, Makeda had Obsessive Compulsive Disorder. She did not like a thing out of their place. She cleaned my room all the time, so I left her to the task.

I jumped in the shower and used my Honey and Ginger Exfoliating Scrub by Knatural Kreations and cleaned all my parts vigorously. By the time I got out of the shower, all of my clothes had been put away, and the outfit she chose for me was laid out neatly on my bed, including the headband. I grab my Mint Lemongrass shea butter, and I slather my body with the luxurious blend. Then proceeded to my panty drawer and grab a set.

Once my underwear was on, I began the process of getting dressed. Once completely clothed, I stood in the mirror and took my Bantu knots down. I fingered through the curl pattern lightly. I wanted the curls to be big and full. I grabbed my lip balm and moisturized my lips and used a little eyeliner to make my pretty brows pop. Satisfied with my appearance, I wen in my closet and grabbed a flowered tote bag I'd purchased from Target and filled it will all of the essentials a girl needed, and I made my way down our stairs. When I got to the living room, I saw Makeda sitting across Fahrice, giving him the third degree.

"What type of childhood did you have? Where your parents married or co-parenting? How do you feel about your mother? Are women your equals or your subordinates? Do you work? How much money do you have in your savings? Can you fight? What do you want with my sister?"

Each question Makeda fired off, Fahrice's face grew a little redder. As amusing as it was to see him squirming in the hot seat; I knew if I didn't save him, Makeda would probably give the poor guy a heart attack. I stepped into the living room, and everyone turned my way.

"Makeda, that's enough. I apologize for my twin, Fahrice. She can be a little intense."

"Sissy, I was trying to get a feel for the man. I wasn't going to hurt him, just a little friendly conversation. It's not every day that my baby sister goes on her first date," Makeda said, and immediately, I became embarrassed. The damn girl was born thirty seconds ahead of me.

"Nefertiti, you look simply amazing. I am glad to be the first, for it's a pleasure to have you accompany me, tonight," Fahrice complimented me while giving me an all-consuming look that ignited my senses.

"Oh hell, he is a smooth talker. Nefertiti, don't be a fast ass and remember no means no. Goodnight, folks. Oh, and Fahrice, if my sister comes back home with even an eyelash missing, I will come to snatch your spleen through your urethra. No pressure." With that statement, Makeda exited the living room, and I was left standing next to Fahrice, shaking my head.

"Don't feel embarrassed. It's a good thing to know that you are loved," Fahrice said as if he could read the emotions across my face.

"Yeah, you're right. Sometimes, too much. Well, I'm excited to get this show on the road. Where are we going?" I asked him as I led him to the front door to grab my jean jacket.

"I was thinking since we have so much fun playing games online that we can go to Dave and Buster's and play in person," Fahrice responded, and that tipped my excitement off the Richter scales.

"I have always wanted to go there. It feels like our first date is going to be so amazing."

"I know, I remember you were telling me that, and it's on my bucket list, so here we are."

He led me over to his Lexus ES 350 and opened my door. I slid into the passenger seat, and then leaned over to open his door. I remembered reading on Google that it was a custom in romantic social situations. I sat back in my seat and buckled up. Fahrice climbed in, and when he started the car, I heard John Coltrane's My Favorite Things album playing. The whole ride to the restaurant, I grooved to the jazz instrumental, from one of the greatest jazz musicians to ever grace the world.

We arrived at our destination, and I almost didn't want to leave the vibe of the car. The music was so soothing, and although we didn't waste space with mundane chatter, I still felt him. Fahrice kept up with his gentlemanly manner, as he came around my side to open the door. He then lent me a hand and helped me out of the car.

He never let my hand go as he led me inside of Dave and Buster's. We got to the front where we were carded, and then headed over to the supercharge kiosks where Fahrice added money to cards, so we could play. With those cards in our hands, we went out onto the floor and commenced a night of true gaming fun.

We played Pop-A-Shot, Pac-Man, and Skee-Ball. Then I battled him in Dance Dance Revolution, where I got the shock of my life because Fahrice had all the moves and easily showed me up on the game. I redeemed myself by kicking his ass at Dragon Frost VR, and we ended the night with drinks and conversation over bowling. Now it was time to leave the place that became a new memory.

As we were leaving, I began to feel sluggish, so I sat on a bench outside the restaurant, and Fahrice joined me. All of those snacks, wings, and treats I consumed were catching up to me. I yawned really big and covered my mouth.

"Somebody is sleepy, I see."

"Yes, please excuse me. I feel like my limbs have weights on them. It's been a while since I indulged in so much comfort food."

"Would you like to walk it off? The pier is just around the corner, and we can sit and watch the boats. Maybe the good breeze coming off of the Delaware River can awaken your senses." Fahrice was enthusiastically asking me to extend our date, and it was too cute. Although it sounded good in theory, I knew nothing was going to stop the need for sleep that was jonesing in my bones from happening.

"That's a very good idea, but I would like to take a rain check. I enjoyed the time we spent, but I'm a whole different animal when I'm tired," I admitted truthfully. Fahrice chuckled and then stood to pull me up off of the bench.

"In that case, I should get you home, so you can conserve your beauty." It was corny, but I laughed from the gut.

He placed his arm around my shoulder and drew me against his body. We walked in companionable silence until we reached his car. After allowing me entrance, I got inside, and he rushed around to his side. We pulled off, and I felt all of the fun we had, fall over my body like a rushing tide. At that point, I was struggling to keep my head up. When he cut the radio on, I exploded into a fit of giggles at his musical selection to accompany us on the way back to my house. Fahrice was playing old school Jeezy, and I'm talking Thug Motivation old. It was funny watching him sitting there, rapping to *Last of a Dying Breed,* and I was shocked when he started performing for me.

Comment [KF]: Song titles should be italicized or framed by quotations.

Comment [nF]: I will remember going forard

Comment [nF]:

Fahrice turned to me and smiled while he continued to rap with the flow. I was giggling at him and how urban he appeared as if that was his element. It was the greatest oxymoron I had ever witnessed.

"What are you staring at, girl? A man can't flow in his whip without getting judged."

"Ain't nobody judging you, man. I just find it funny that you are even more of a nerd than me, and yet you're rocking out to gangsta music. Who would have known?"

"Don't hate cause this geek got a little flavor in him. You gone respect all my angles, you dig."

We began joking back and forth, and it was the most carefree I have ever been with anyone outside of my twin. When he pulled up to my house, I got a little sad. I didn't want this fun time to end. He hopped out and came around to my side and helped me out. He placed my hand in his, and we walked to the door. We reached the front of my house, and I turned to him.

"Thank you, Fahrice, for a wonderful time. I'm glad you asked me out."

"The pleasure was all mine, Nefertiti. You were pleasurable company, and I would love to do this again sometime." Fahrice's words were escaping me because his eyes held me transfixed.

Next thing I knew, Fahrice placed both hands on the side of my head and stole my breath with a succulent kiss. At first, we were a bit clumsy in our ministrations. I felt we were overthinking the moment. Then I decided just to let go and give him all the good feelings I'd held inside of me. Then, Fahrice took over the kiss and became aggressive but soft at the same time.

His lips felt like down-filled pillows, and they could easily become my favorite sleep aid. When he pulled back, it took a moment for my mind to realize we'd stopped sharing life forces. If my hands weren't gripping his elbows, I would have fallen on my face. I'd never felt this lost but aware at the same time.

It took me a minute to finally open my eyes. When my oculars focused, Fahrice was staring at me with dilated pupils and a raging heartbeat. His look obliterated me, and the resulting feeling was foreign. Never in my life had a man look at me in a manner that made me feel exposed but safe. It felt as if the promise in his eyes would lead to do dangerous things that I'd never considered, and that scared me. So, I stepped out of his arms and tried to use the space to gain clarity. Particularly, because my soul was begging me to invite him inside, and I didn't know what was to happen after that. Since inviting him in felt like a natural inclination, I wanted to avoid it with the appropriate objectivity.

"Goodnight, Fahrice. Be sure to call me when you make it home."

"Goodnight, beautiful, until the next time we speak."

He waited like a gentleman while I entered the house before he left the porch and headed to his car. I rushed to my front window and watched him drive away. Shivers ran down my spine as I stood there long after he left. All I could think was that I would see much more of Fahrice. My heart had been opened for the first time, and I want to follow that feeling wherever he led me.

## Chapter 10: Isis

The last three months had gone by in a whirlwind of activity. I went from being Isis Torrance to Mrs. Fabian Moore. A title that I wore with copious amounts of pride. It was like the most fulfilling role I'd ever taken on. It made my first time around, pale in comparison. This time, I felt like a real wife with a true sense of duty, and it was all for a man who loved my dirty draws and didn't mind showing the world. That was why today, we were in the bank, so that I could show him how much I was committed to this life we'd created together

"Ms. Torrance, are you sure about adding an authorized user with no restrictions? There is a substantial amount of money in all of these accounts, and it would be in your best interest to put a dual authorization, or at the very minimum, spending and transferring restrictions. If we do this, he will have the same level of authorization as you, and we would advise against that action," the customer service representative at the bank said by way of warning, and her opinion was unwarranted.

"I'm well aware of what I'm asking you to do. I don't need your advice or misguided direction concerning my affairs. He, as you called him, is my husband. That means that what's mine is also his. I didn't ask for a counselor, now add him to the accounts, and that is your only job. Oh, yeah, my last name is Moore, so be sure to update that as well."

Fabian was looking at me with the utmost respect mixed with desire. It felt amazing anytime I got his approval. The bank was our third stop of the day and the most frustrating. We had already been to my attorney's office to get his name added to all of the paperwork for my businesses and added him to my updated will. From there, we went down to the registrar of wills to add his name on the deed to my house. My new marriage was my last chance at love, and it would be till death do us part, literally. I wasn't playing any games nor taking any shorts.

I gave the representative a copy of our marriage license along with my new photo ID and social security card. She took all of my information, plus his identifying documents, and set about the task of merging our finances. After we signed all of the paperwork, Fabian chose the password for his temporary card, then got up and pulled my chair back. I stood, and he took my hand in his, and then my king led me out of the bank.

Once outside, we hopped in Fabian's Denali truck. His truck was one of the many wedding gifts that I'd bestowed upon him. He opened my door and helped me to climb inside. As I ascended into the truck, I felt a stinging smack on my ass. I looked over my shoulder, and Fabian stood there, biting his lip as if he wanted to eat me up. He'd better stop playing with me because he knew I would bust it open in the middle of the parking lot for a real nigga. It was my job to keep my man's belly full and his nutsack empty, and I never failed at my duties.

"Gon' ahead, woman, and sit down. I'm not about to play with your freaky ass today. We will be taking this moment back to the crib, where I can flip that ass upside down while you suck this dick." My eyes lit up with amusement as he went around to his side of the truck and got in. He knew not to threaten me with a good time.

"Shit, I've been practicing my handstand, so you not about to make me tap out today."

That made Fabian guffaw at my attempt to talk shit. We played a game often, where Fabian tried to see if I could make him bust a nut before I get dangerously lightheaded. So far, I'd always been on the losing end but, I wasn't lying when I said I'd been practicing. Fabian was going to learn today.

"Whatever woman, you're always too stubborn to give up. Last time, your nose bled all over the carpet and scared the shit out of me."

"Fuck this nose! My job isn't finished until you cum. The question is, did I die?"

"Woman, you're crazy as shit."

Fabian was out of breath from laughing at my theatrics, but he knew I was dead serious. My philosophy was; I would never leave room for another woman to think she can be my man's side bitch. After all the fucking and sucking we did, Fabian would never have any energy to entertain a slide. I played for keeps, and Fabian is was one of my prized possessions.

I was staring at my husband's side profile with the adoration of an obsessed creep, and he must have felt my eyes. He turned away from the road and procccdcd to makc goofy faces at me, which had me all cheesed up from his attention. I took my hand and placed it upon his head and began to run my fingers through his curls. With that same hand, I moved down and started tugging and fiddling in his beard. The motion was soothing to me as I enjoyed this silence between us.

We got off at the exit that led to our home. The closer we got, the more anxious I became. Our earlier conversation in the parking lot had me excited to get home and get to the action. We pulled up to the gate, and he input the code. The drive down our two-mile-long driveway had me about to say fuck getting to the house. He was going to have to take me down in the car.

"Woman, if you don't stop all that hot pussy bouncing. We like a hundred feet from the house."

"Hurry the hell up, so I can put this bounce all over your dick."

I'd been so focused on the dick; I didn't notice that he slowed down or that he never responded to my invitation. Fabian had a strange look on his face, and his eyes were laser-focused, staring out of the windshield. I whipped my head in that direction to see what had his dedicated attention.

There, in front of our home, stood my daughters. Them being there wouldn't normally be shocking, except Makeda was pacing back and forth with two Glock 30s, and Nefertiti was casually slouched against her car with her favorite nine millimeter and elbows on the hood as if she didn't have a care in the world.

"Oh shit," I said out loud, and that set Fabian off.

"What the hell is going on? Who are these ladies trespassing on our property? Why do they have guns?" I didn't want to answer him, but I did out of respect.

"Those are my daughters. Please, let me handle this. Don't get out of the car."

Where did I begin with how to explain this to either my children or my husband? They'd never met each other, and this was not how I'd planned to break the news. Fabian and I had been so caught up in our feelings and just enjoying each other, and it was as if the outside world didn't exist. Now, I had to diffuse the situation because I knew my children, and they would start airing it out without any questions asked.

"Makeda, why are you outside my house ready for war?" I asked as if I was clueless, and that automatically sent Makeda over the edge.

"Isis Superiority Torrence, today, is not the day you're gon' play with me. I don't even know where to begin with you or your philistinism. All I know is I'm ready to start killing shit. Nefertiti, please talk to your mother before I make her go, poof." I knew Makeda had to be out of her rabid ass mind talking to me like I didn't give her the G she was trying to stand on.

"Makeda, you do know who taught you how to shoot. I'm not scared of you or your little baby threats. Somebody better get to fucking telling what the issue is, since bitches want to be calling me outside my title like I won't put motherfuckers back inside the womb."

I didn't care what they thought I did or that I knew I was wrong. No child of mine would ever disrespect me openly like I wouldn't put them in a ditch with not a fuck to give. It may not make sense to anyone else, but I said what I said. Makeda could act crazy all she wanted to, and I would body her out here and cry at her funeral.

"Mom, first of all, you've been missing in action, and only texting like that's sufficient enough. We have only seen you twice in the last month. Now today, every security alert that I placed on your accounts and the business accounts showed not only that you have added an authorized user, but you changed your last name. You have to tell us something. Decisions like that need to be discussed."

I stared at Nefertiti because out of all she said, the only thing I heard was that she called me Mom instead of Mommy. I tried to gather my thoughts and formulate a statement. Then I felt my husband's arms wrap around me. He kissed the side of my face then did something I hoped he would never do. That's why I asked him to stay in the car.

"If I may interject, you girls coming here to question your mother, about things that don't concern you, doesn't sit well with me. She is your parent, and she doesn't owe you any explanations. As my wife, the only one she will ever answer to, is me. Now, you all can come into our home and talk civilized, or you can remove yourselves from our property." My head was shaking no, vigorously. Fabian didn't know what he just started, and that was not how you approached my young.

That damn Makeda's head leaned to the side so strong, I thought she was getting low. I felt my heart tremble because she was my child, and she was not just with the shits--she *was* the shits.

"Bitch ass nigga, don't you in all of your clap on, clap off, light bright in the dark playing ass life, ever address me or my sister concerning a bitch, whose pussy we did the electric slide out of into the world. I'm not sure if you're aware of who I am but let me make you privy. I'm not a safe topic, and you gon' want to do something else besides putting your dicksuckers together to formulate a check because I'm un-checkable, bitch!

"You have to be smoking hella dicks, to ever try to use your Cartman from south park, respect my authority ass voice and think you moved something. I will move your mama wig back a couple of inches from worry. Playing with me, I will put yo ass in a ditch and pay for your homegoing, so I can come spit on you in peace. Nefertiti, let's go before I show these motherfuckers the definition of till death do them part."

I could only put my head down. I felt a severe migraine coming on. Makeda hopped in the driver's seat, and Nefertiti turned around and gave us one of her signature creepy smiles. That sent chills down my spine because people underestimated Nefertiti because she was the quiet one. I knew better. That girl was twenty-two shades of crazy.

"Hey, punk-ass stepdaddy, we shall see you around. Stay safe out here because there are things that go bang-bang in the night."

I turned to look at my husband, and he looked a little bit green in the face. His eyes showed malice, and concerning my kids, he was gone need to find a different emotion. I pushed

95

him right in the chest, ready to kick off a war about my disrespectful offspring. Nobody in life could give me flavor about nor show and type of disgust, contempt, hate, or animosity toward mine and think I wouldn't push their muffin back.

"Why are you looking at my children leaving like that? You got a beef with mine, tell me now because I can cook that up. You want it rare or well-done?"

"Why are you talking to me crazy after your children disrespected me, in front of our home, because I was trying to defend my wife?" Fabian asked as if he didn't step into an arena no one invited him to. His actions may have just kicked off a war, and he didn't see the fallacy in his course of action. Well, it was time I gave him a reality check.

"You don't have to protect me from shit that I nurtured inside my body for ten months and pushed out. They are not my enemy. They had a right to feel that way, and I would have answered their questions and introduced you to them, on my terms. I don't need a man ever to step in and try to check my kids about nothing. That was not your place to do that, so you were dead wrong." I spelled it out for him since he wanted to pretend to be slow.

"That's the fucking point, Isis. Why don't your children know about me, or that you are not only rocking my ring but my last name? Like what the fuck are we even doing? Are you ashamed of me or something? I'm trying to figure out how my wife, my life, and everything sat on the sidelines and let me get disrespected, then took it a step further and told me how much I was not needed. So, what's the point of being here? I married you to join our lives, not to still feel like an outsider. Thanks for opening my eyes to what I truly am to you."

With that statement, he walked into the house. I stood outside just stuck in place with a heavy heart. I didn't know what the fallout would be from today, but I knew I had to bring my family together. The thought of losing my husband shook my soul. How did I keep my dreams without hurting my babies? All I knew was that letting my husband walk away wasn't an option, and losing my children was non-negotiable.

## Chapter 11: Makeda

I was .38 hot, and it was going to take herculean power to get me to calm down. There was no understanding of where my mother got the nerve, the audacity, or the gall to ever play in our faces. Ever since we pulled up on her and her "alleged" husband, I had been in my bag. All I wanted to do was lay motherfucker's down until my animosity dissipated. That was why I was glad to be on a job that took me out of town. It was necessary to put space between my mother and me, before I forgot she ever spit me out of her rotten pussy.

When we made it to the house that night, I got ghost on my sister. I didn't want to see or speak to anybody until the inferno inside of me died down. My closet, or more specifically, what's inside of the closet, was calling my name, and I readily answered. When I opened the doors, I pushed a button, and my clothes parted like the red sea, and my pride and joy came forward.

There in front of me was my collection of guns. Although I specialized in poison and hand-to-hand combat when it came to my company, it was something about the power behind a gun that made my blood flow a little harder. Guns were not my weapons of choice because it left more of a mess than I could stomach. They served their purpose when I was angry or working through my thoughts — the smell of gun powder and the adrenaline from firing weapons, helped me center my thinking.

I'd taken a moment to peruse the shelves, trying to decide on which one would help me through my latest issues. I decided on the MPA Grim Reaper Defender 9 mm Luger Semi-Auto Pistol. It shot thirty rounds with a six-inch Threaded Barrel and Threaded 1/2x28 TPI. I'd had it customized to extend the clip to sixty rounds for purposes like this. After grabbing a few other guns, extra clips, and a bag to tote them all, I prepared to go put in work.

I took the elevator in my room down to the basement. In the basement, we built a special shooting course just for me. I stepped off the elevator and entered the course, taking a moment to survey my surroundings. The room was soundproof, but I went to the wall and clicked the "Do Not Disturb" light outside the door. If I knew my twin, she would find her way to me, and I didn't need the distraction.

I'd grabbed a set of headphones off the wall, and I used my phone and pulled up my trap mix on Spotify. I picked up my weapon and let the sounds of Jeezy take me into the first moments of my workout. With my mind focused, I let the first bullets rip through my target.

Every target I encountered got one to the head and two to the chest. I was eight targets in before my limbs started to relax. By target twenty, I'd begun rationalizing the catalyst of my current mood and thoughts. Love was slowly poisoning the people around me.

Nefertiti, who was already reclusive, had become even more so since she started dating Fahrice. She'd begun missing our sister nights, and we barely talked anymore. If she wasn't on the phone with him, they were busy playing online games. When I was away on an assignment, I'd only heard from her regarding the job, and that was not like us. We constantly talked, and for some reason, her limited conversation made me resent this new person she'd become. It was as if all she saw was that light-skinned bastard, and I hated that with a passion.

Then, my mom had the nerve to go and secretly get married. It wasn't even the fact that she found someone to spend her life with; it was all of the secrecy behind the union. It had only been us forever, and one thing my mother had never done, was lie to us. The fact she felt the need to do so, let me know that it was bullshit. Now that her supposed husband had rubbed me the wrong way, I didn't feel whatever their situation was, and he had better hope he wasn't another number on my hitlist.

I'd worked up a sweat, and Jeezy's album had played through twice. That was enough of a workout for me so, I took my headphones off and prepared to go back up to my room and ruminate some more. When I reached the beginning of the obstacle course, my sister was sitting there with headphones on reading a book. She didn't notice me, and I had no rap, so I walked passed her like she was invisible.

Before I made it to the door, I felt something slam into the back of my head before clunking onto the floor. When I looked down, I saw a book, and when I turned around, a raging Nefertiti stood behind me.

"Why would you throw your dumbass book at me?" I asked Nefertiti's childish ass.

"Why would you pretend not to see me sitting there, waiting for you to get done?" Nefertiti rebutted, and I wasn't about to sit there and entertain her reasoning.

"Because I don't see you. What was your purpose for coming down here anyway? The door said, "Do Not Disturb," but yet you brought your stupid ass in here, and now you want to throw objects at me on some goofy shit. Leave me the fuck alone, Nefi."

"How dare you. You have been walking around here with a chip on your shoulder. I know you are mad at Mommy, but I've done nothing to you and don't know why you are taking it out on me."

"Oh, now you notice that something is wrong. I mean, you have finally pulled your head out of that nigga's ass, and now what I feel or don't is important. Just leave me alone because I don't have time for your wishy-washy ass or your mother's sneaky, creepy pussy. Fuck y'all and fuck love. I don't matter anymore to anybody, so just *leave me alone!*"

My body was vibrating with anger, and for the first time in years, tears had slipped from my eyes and graced my cheeks. Nefertiti had come and wrapped me up in her arms, and it made my deep soul of misery shatter. Nobody cared that I was lonely as hell, and my family had been the only thing that sheltered me from having to feel the pain caused by loneliness. It used to be us against the world, and because of them finding new affections, I was the odd man out. I wanted them to take it back to how it used to be before they found others to love, instead of me. If I couldn't find the complacency of normalcy, I wasn't going to survive loneliness or its effects.

"Sissy, you are important to all of us. I'm sorry if you feel like since we've found mates that you're insignificant. Love doesn't change the fact that our bond reaches past our soul. No one could ever take your place. Yes, I've been preoccupied because learning, to love someone has been like studying for a new degree. There are so many things to explore, and it has been all-consuming, and for that, I apologize. Watching you breakdown like this is making me feel very shitty as your twin. What can I do to make this better?"

"Let's kill them, and then it will be just us again." My suggestion made Nefertiti chuckle.

"No, sissy, we have to be adults about this. What I will do is arrange a sit down with our mother, and we can talk about the changes that are going on in our lives, and then we can figure out how to protect our relationships without casualties."

We pulled apart, and then hand-in-hand, we went up to my room. For the rest of the night, my twin doted on me. Nefertiti, cut her phone off, and we watched movies, and even talked in-depth about our mom's marriage. We came to the consensus that there was definitely something fishy with the whole rushed marriage and hiding spouses. We would get to the bottom of it all, and for his sake, everything had better check out, or we would check his life in.

## Chapter 12: Pierre

"Bitch, I'm sick of you! You can't do shit right. How hard is it to make fried chicken?" I was yelling as I viscously stomped a mudhole in my incompetent ass baby mama.

"Pierre, please stop! I will get up recook the chicken. Please, stop kicking me. I can't take it anymore!"

I didn't know why she was wasting her breath, begging me when she knew how this went. Her whining and crying were making me madder, so I started trying to knock her brain loose with these haymakers. I heard my front door open and close, and there stood my son, my namesake, walking by. He stopped momentarily to stare at me, and I returned his stare with all the venom in my body, hoping it scared him into minding his business. My son didn't even blink, so I took that as a personal affront.

"What the fuck you looking at, little nigga? You want some of what she's getting?" His laughter wasn't the reaction I'd expected in response to my threat.

"You better play with something safe, old nigga. You know I will mangle ya mitts like I did last time. The only person scared of you is that bitch you're stomping into the ground. One day soon, you won't be able to do that, and that's on me."

He said that shit, and then walked off to his room. What he said sent a chill down my spine, so much so, I dropped his worthless ass mother on the floor and walked away. My son and I had a bitter relationship. He hated me for what I did to his mother, and he hated his mother for allowing me to continue breaking her down.

I remembered the first time that he stepped up in defense of his mother. He had to be about fifteen, and I guess he got tired of me closing her eyes for weeks at a time or her endless nights and days of crying. This particular fight; my baby mama had blacked out from all the hits she took to the head. As I stood there trying to wake her up, thinking she was playing possum, that little motherfucker came from his nuts and gave me major smoke. We tore my house the fuck up, and I damn near had a heart attack trying to match the power of his youth. For every punch I threw, he would throw three, and it was then that I knew he would be a problem.

After that night, if I beat his mother ass, he would come to her rescue. It was that way until he was seventeen, when he knocked me out after one of our many rumbles. I mean, a nigga was sleep so hard that when I came to, it felt like I'd been in a coma. What I didn't know was that when he knocked me out, his mother came to my defense and went upside his head with a broomstick. That day, he vowed never to defend a bitch, who loved to get her head knocked off more than she loved her son.

I headed into my downstairs bathroom and washed the blood off of my hands. After they were clean, I'd noticed there was bruising, but it was all in a day's work. If I was honest with myself, I was tired of living in the nightmare called my life. Whipping my baby mama's ass was not fulfilling anymore, but I didn't know how else to make her pay.

I met Naira right after I'd found out that Isis was giving me daughters. I was wilding out in the streets and trying to live with the disappointment, no matter how displaced, that my wife had failed me. One night, I ended up at a college party, where I laid eyes on Naira, and she was beautiful. She had flawless brown skin and curly hair. You could tell from her eyes that she was mixed with a little something. I placed my mack game down, and she was in love at first sight.

I found out Naira was in the last semester of her senior year in college. We vibed heavy; from her intellect down to her freakiness. It started out with me wanting to smash and ended up turning into a twisted love story. The whole time I was dealing with her, she never knew that I had a wife and children at home.

I still went home to my wife every now and then. Isis was not one to be easily forgotten. Missing my wife was natural, but I could never forgive her for giving me daughters. So, I would slide in late at night and be gone before those little disappointments woke up. For a while, I went between the two, and I was living on top of the world. Then, Naira came and changed the game.

Naira told me she found out she was pregnant, and she was about four months along. I didn't know how to take the news, so I cut her off. All I knew was I couldn't take another disappointment. That was until months later when she showed up to the hood with a baby, and the baby was a boy. I remembered crying and jumping for joy and thinking that I knew Isis's womb had to have been corrupted. The day after Niara gave me my son, I filed for divorce. Isis didn't contest anything and asked me for nothing.

Comment [KF]: Please verify character's name. The initial spelling was Naira.

On the day it was finalized, I packed up Naira and Pierre Jr. and took them to my house. Why shouldn't my true queen have a mansion to live in, when she birth the only heir to my throne? I didn't care if Isis and her daughters were still there. I was tired of hiding my real family. Naira gave me a namesake, and I intended to give her the world. We pulled up to my crib just as Isis and the girls were coming outside. Like the arrogant bastard that I was, my family and I got out of the car as if we belonged there. I wanted Isis to see my son and my new happiness since she couldn't give it to me.

Isis stared right at me like I was the shit beneath her shoe. She didn't even flinch, and she stood before us, uncaring. One of those little girls ran up on me and tried to hug me. I pushed it right back as if she would taint me. When I did that, it was like I could see a war brewing in her eyes. The fire from that gaze should have incinerated me. We stood in the intense stare-off, and Isis vowed to make me feel her. Her threats meant nothing to me because I lived my life carefree and in fear of no one.

You couldn't tell me shit, and Naira never questioned me about the strange woman or the children with her. Niara was only concerned with being put on the pedestal that I built. Until one day, I woke up in a dream world. My traps were taken over, my connect changed his number, my homies acted like they never knew me, no one feared me, and I became a has-been. It was also the day I started whipping Naira's ass for breakfast, lunch, and dinner. I equated her as the beginning of my downfall, and I held that animosity until the present day.

If I weren't smart about my money, I would have probably been dead broke. I had millions of dollars saved spread around different offshore accounts and a few legit businesses. It took about five years for me to realize I was just a regular square. All I did was work my businesses and pay my taxes. I no longer had notoriety or street credibility. It was an existence that I loathed with every fiber of my being.

I walked into my bedroom, and Naira was sitting at her vanity nursing her wounds. In the beginning, I felt remorse. Now, I felt like she provoked me on purpose, so her injuries were her fault. I sat on the bed and placed my head in my hands. My life was just so fucked up, and in a minute, it wouldn't be. I heard my phone ringing, and when I pick up, it was just the call I'd been waiting to receive.

"Hello, hold on a sec," I told the caller and stepped out of the room into the hallway. When I got there, I put the phone back to my ear.

"Yo, man what's cooking?"

"Man, this shit is almost complete, and you don't even understand how hard this shit is getting for me. It almost was an aborted mission when your daughter decided she wanted to pull a gun on me. I wanted to snap her neck." Fabian was on the line complaining.

"That little bitch ain't my daughter. You would have been better off killing her. How much longer do you think you need before we can kill Isis?"

"Man, that little shit show with her daughter set us a little off track. I almost lost my life, but Isis has been giving me the cold shoulder. I will probably have to kiss her ass to get her back under my spell. I'm not built for the extra effort it's taking to get this bitch to give me her life," Fabian sounded exasperated, but I didn't need him to fold when we were so close.

"Listen to me, man, whatever you have to do to get it accomplished, please do. I can't wait for the day I can make her pay me back with her life. All you need to do is get her to sign the papers, and we will ride off into the sunset--rich as fuck-- and the world will be free from this worthless bitch."

"I agree. I have to go in here and make this shit right with her. If she didn't have some good pussy, my job would be a lot harder. I have to pay my son, Fahrice, a visit and see why he hasn't been answering my calls. I need him to get me that paperwork or none of this will be worth anything."

"Go put your foot on his neck, then. We can't afford any mistakes. That paperwork is what stands between us and taking Isis down permanently."

We said our goodbyes, and I stood there with a goofy grin on my face. That was until I turned around and saw my son standing there. I damn near jumped out of my skin. Pulling my composure back together; I act cool, calm, and collected.

"Why you just standing there in the hallway like a weirdo? Did you need something?" I asked.

"Naw, I wasn't standing here. I'm just passing through on my way out," he responded and walked away.

When he was gone, I breathed a sigh of relief. I was glad to know he wasn't privy to my conversation. That would have gone bad real quick. I headed back into my room, and Naira was in bed lying down. I dropped my pants and boxers and climbed in beside her. I started kissing on her neck and playing in her pussy, and she assumed the position. I closed my night out by putting this dick in her life and dreaming of the demise of my past.

# Chapter 13: Fahrice

All I wanted to do was get home and get in my bed. It was hard being a young genius because I was always asked to give lectures and assist professors in teaching. Sometimes, I wanted to live a normal life and kick my heels up and have fun. It was why I loved the relationship between Nefertiti and myself. She understood me on a level, not even my blood relations could comprehend.

We could talk about the intricacies of technology and how it would change the world or simply our favorite comic books. Nefertiti's mind was just as beautiful and full as mine and that had me enraptured with her being. Nefertiti was on my brain so heavy that using Bluetooth, I called out to Siri and told her to facetime "My little Einstein." The phone in the holder on my dash did as I commanded and shortly after that, Nefertiti's face appeared on the screen.

"Hey baby, where are you?" she asked me

"I just made it back into town. I was thinking of you and needed to see your pretty smile."

"Awwww, babe. Did you have fun at the camp for the children of Brilliant Minds?"

"Man, it was so amazing. I promise you, I learned so much from those little innovative people. I'm so glad Mr. Sterling Carter invited me out there. It was a joy to give back to the same program that helped cultivate my ideas and pushed the limits of my mind. I can't wait for you to meet him. He is my greatest mentor, and the best influence of my life."

"I can't wait to meet him, either. You gotta tell me how to volunteer at the center." I smiled when she said that. Nefertiti was always driven to give back to the community whenever she could.

"I will send you the link, and when you're done, I will call Mr. Carter and let him know to pull your app."

"I missed you, babe. I needed a hug a few days ago." When she said that, I felt her sadness come through the line.

"What happened? Do you need me to come there now?" I asked with genuine concern because attending to Nefertiti's needs was a priority.

"No, babe. I'm okay. Don't come out of your way. I know how you like to go home and decompress after you travel."

"But babe, I want to be there for you in any way you need me to be. Coming to you is not an inconvenience, it's my job."

"That's why I love you. You take care of me in so many ways."

"I love you more, beautiful. Since you don't want me to come, tell me what's wrong?"

"It's my mom. We got all of these alerts that she authorized a new user on all of her accounts and businesses. She has even changed her last name. We already been worried about her since she has not been coming around, nor has she been responsive to our calls and texts.

"Thinking the worst, we showed up to her house for a bit of a chat to see what was up with the changes. I don't know how long we waited, and Makeda paced until she showed up, and we could get to the bottom of the mystery.

Only she wasn't alone, and in the middle of our family dispute, her husband decided to get in the middle of our family battle. He was this older, light-skinned dude with the same funny looking eyes as you but without the green. His input made Makeda snap. We haven't talked to her since then, and it just feels all wrong.

"I, more than Makeda, am a momma's girl, not that she doesn't love her to death, but my mom's and my relationship is different. I came home that night and tried to search for this man, and I found nothing. It's like he is straight up and down on paper. I don't trust it because his eyes told me he meant my mother no good. Do you think you can look him up for me?"

When she gets done her story, I felt my heart drop. It was like déjà vu, and I continued listening to her, hoping she didn't notice the change in my disposition. If she was talking about whom I thought she was, then Nefertiti didn't understand it was only the beginning. I feel my anxiety skyrocketing because it was a possibility that my secrets might have come back to bite me in the ass. What I felt for Nefertiti was genuine, but when the shit hit the fan, my actions would undoubtedly make me look guilty. I was pulling up to my driveway and saw the absolute last person in the world I wanted to see. It shouldn't surprise me because I knew he would eventually come, since things weren't running as smoothly as before.

"Baby, let me call you right back. I love you."

I'd hung up on Nefertiti before she could respond and exited my vehicle. When I got to the front of my car, I stood against it casually. I stared into the eyes that were like mine, except they were cold and lifeless. Ever since he caught my mother cheating on him when he was overseas, fighting a pointless war, he had never been the same. As his offspring, you could only imagine the life I lived without the love of my mother, and the product of the heart she damaged.

"What can I do for you, Fabian?" I'd wasted no time getting to the point because any moment with my father sucked away my joy.

"I'm trying to figure out why you have been ducking me. You know how this thing I do goes. I get the referral, and you handle the paperwork. If not for that, I wouldn't even be here, son." His calling me son, had the anger rising from my toes to the crown of my head.

"Listen, I told you that the last assignment was the last project, I would ever do for you. I gave you a referral, months ago, to another hacker that could do all of your dirty work, but you insist on oppressing me. None of this is funny anymore, and I won't keep compromising my morals just so you…"

"You're done, when the fuck I say you're done. You must not remember what is at stake for you. It will take nothing for me to make a phone call and have your brother killed. So, if you want him to continue breathing, then you will help me finish this last assignment, then I will let your bitch ass brother go free."

I ran my hands through my hair because this is why I stay stressed. The day I graduated from Morehouse with the highest-grade point average ever recorded, and they certified me as a genius, was the day Fabian decided that the college education his military training paid for was going to be for his gain. He approached me about his little hustle of scamming women out of their money. He told me that I needed to use my talents to help him get even with all the corrupt women in the world. I politely declined, and I would pay dearly for that stand of morality.

When I woke up the next day, Fabian, my brother, Fahraad, and my sister, Mikayla, were gone. He told me that if I ever wanted to see my brother again, that I would accept his proposition. I was distraught because Fahraad was Autistic. He only talked to me, and I was his safe haven. He knew that by taking Fahraad, it would possibly trigger him to have a violent episode and being separated from me would drive him crazy. My back was against the wall, and I loved my brother more than life.

Of course, I deluded myself into thinking that the first time would be the only time. Nope, over the last eight years or so, I had helped Fabian destroy more than a few lives, and I hated doing this because it was not how I wanted to use my gift. If I had not witnessed his evil firsthand, I might have risked going rogue. The love of my brother kept me his puppet, and his evil ass felt no remorse at my ire. I had to figure out how to turn the odds in my favor. I walked past him and headed into my apartment building. No one knew that I owned this place, and no one else lived there but me.

I knew Fabian was following behind me, so I don't even look back. I raced up to the fifth floor, scanned my palm and let him inside. He took a seat, and I turn around to him.

"Name of the target, and what phase of the plan are you in?"

"Isis Torrence, and we are in the end game."

"Okay, I will be right back."

I headed into a separate room where I kept all of the files of his victims. Picking up the file with her name, I opened it and read it for the first time. This client was a referral, and I usually ran a check and printed the information to be sure that the person was correct. Once they let me know that this is the target, I would email Fabian a full docket and file a hard copy for my sanity and not bear witness to his unsuspecting victim.

Inside I saw pics that I printed of her, and then I ran across two birth certificates and other papers — one for Makeda and Nefertiti, listing Isis Torrence as their mother. Now, Nefertiti's story was coming back, and now, it all made sense. What the fuck! This just couldn't be happening. If he was at the end game, then he was about to have her sign over her whole life, thinking that she was merely signing papers to add her to all of his fortunes. I had to think quickly and turn the tables around. I couldn't allow Fabian to hurt my future wife or her family in this manner. I grabbed the file and went back out to where Fabian was still seated. I sat at my computer and started to open up the needed documents.

"I just have to put your names in the document, so give me a moment." Fabian didn't acknowledge my statement with anything other than a nod as he was preoccupied with his phone.

I use that moment of distraction to go into the document and make some addendums. Once finished, I started printing out the documents. I gathered them from the printer and placed them in an official-looking folder. When done, I walked over to Fabian and cleared my throat to grab his attention.

"I have the documents right here. Before I hand these over to you, I want to know that our debt is clear, and that I'm officially done with your schemes. All I want is my brother and to live my life free and clear," I told Fabian with seriousness.

"Okay, you little cry baby ass nigga. I don't know how you came out of my nutsack. Give me the papers," he said while trying to snatch them from me, but I moved out of his reach.

"Nope, before I give you anything, let me talk to my brother. I want to make sure he is still safe." Fabian blew out an exasperated breath before he lifted his phone and facetimed Fahraad. He turned the camera my way.

"Bonjour frère, tu me manques tellement (Hello, brother I miss you so much)," Fahraad said to me in French. He was twenty-one and could speak seven languages even though he was autistic. When we talked, he used different ones, so Fabian could never follow our conversation

"Ne vous inquiétez pas, nous serons bientôt réunis (Don't worry, we will be reunited soon)."

"Hsnana, 'urjuk la tejbny huna (Okay, please hurry. I don't like it here)." Fahraad then switched to Arabic.

"Sayakun 'asrae mimaa taetaqid (It will be sooner than you think)," I responded, and my anxiety was spiking again.

"Addio fratello ti amo (Goodbye brother, I love you)," he spoke in Italian, and then disconnected the video chat.

"You happy? Now, give me the papers. After this, I'm retiring to an island. I can't wait to give him back and be done with all of you. The only one that remotely acts like me is your sister, and she is not even mine. The greatest thing I ever did was to take her from your mother. I molded Mikayla in my image, and I will be glad when it's just her and me." He told me something he had told me forever. At twenty years old, my sister was a corrupt lawyer, who aided my dad in all of his shenanigans.

He took the folder, and then left out of the door. I finally released the breath I'd been holding. I was glad to have him out of my face. My father loved nothing or no one but himself. I only hoped that I did the right thing and didn't risk my brother's life. I picked up my phone and opened my message thread to Nefertiti.

*Me: I need to talk to you. Just know that I love you, and what I share doesn't change anything.*

*My Little Einstein: Okay, meet me at my house in twenty minutes.*

I grab my keys and head back outside. Our conversation would be one that made or broke the relationship, but it was necessary. I could only hope she forgave me and accepted my truth.

# Chapter 14: Fabian

I was getting dressed for this dinner that I put together. Isis thought that this dinner was for the meeting of our families. Little did she know; this is the day I would finally reveal my hand and walk out of there a rich man with no wife. I was jumping up and down with excitement. No one could have told me that six months was all it took to sit on top of the world.

Two months ago,, I had my daughter file the paperwork that I had Isis sign. She thought that I gave her half of all my kingdom, when in all actuality, she signed a living will that stated that if she were to die, I would become sole owner and hold proprietorship over everything she had. All those accounts equaling up into the billions would be mine, along with her businesses and properties. Today was shaping up to be the best day of my life. Especially, since the demise of my wife was pending

I had been slowly feeding Isis arsenic. Tonight, at dinner in front of her siddity daughters and my special guests, I would give her the final lethal dose and watch Olympus fall. I heard her in the bathroom throwing up her guts. I smiled inwardly, but outwardly, I had to play the role of the concerned husband. I rushed into the bathroom while appearing to be in a panic.

"Babe, are you okay?" I said while going to hold her hair while she continued to retch.

When she finished puking, I helped Isis over to the sink, where I passed her the Listerine and a glass of water. She gargled the mouth wash, and then used the water to rinse the after taste. I handed her the towel, and she wiped her face.

"Yeah, I'm okay. It feels like I can't keep anything down. I will be okay in a moment. Would you mind going downstairs and making sure that the caterers are doing their job? I want everything to be perfect. I'm going to jump in the shower and get dressed. I also told Fahraad to go downstairs and sit at the table." I kissed her lips and went to do her bidding for the last time.

When I reached the lower level, Truly Bleu Events had already begun setting up the party. I saw Fahraad sitting at the dining room table with a book in hand that was written in some foreign language. I didn't know how he was born with his brain scrambled but could actually read and speak different languages. He never spoke to me, and I was okay with that. The only person he spoke to was Fahrice, and any other time, he spoke to himself or he remained silent.

I went into the kitchen where the catering owner, Anajma, according to her name tag, was barking orders and setting up displays at the same time. I decided to go to her because she would be instrumental in my plan by ensuring that Isis got the special cup of tea.

"Excuse me, Ms. Anajma, do you have a minute to talk?"

"As long as I don't have to stop working, we are down to the wire, and I can only lend you my ear as my hands are busy."

"Well, I wanted to know if you wouldn't mind putting these vitamins in my wife's wineglass. I have a hard time getting her to take them, and I want to be sure she gets them," I asked while extending the small vial of poison in her direction.

"As fine as you are, you should have just put it on the tip of your dick and fed it to her. But anyway, it's not in my job description to administer medicine, so what you can do is grab a wineglass out of that box, take it and put her required dose in there and sit the glass on top of the fridge. I will be sure to grab it and give it to her. Where will she be seated?" she asked, and that had me getting excited for her deciding to cooperate.

"At the head of the table opposite me."

"Okay, handle your business, but I must get back to work," she told me before heading over to begin working on another display.

Eagerly, I went and grabbed the wineglass. After placing the dose of the poison inside the glass, I sat it on top of the fridge as instructed. I heard the bell ring and with an extra pep in my step, I rushed to answer the door. When I pulled the door open, there stood Isis's daughters, Makeda and Nefertiti. Although I hated these little bitches, I refuse to let it show. I was too happy with my plan panning out to be bothered with trivial emotions.

"Hey, ladies, glad you could make it."

"Whatever, bitch ass nigga, where's my mom?" Makeda said to me, and for three seconds, I imagined how her neck would feel snapped in my hands. I pasted on an even brighter smile because tonight, she would be humbled.

"There is no need for hostilities. We are all family here."

"That's debatable," Nefertiti retorted, and they proceeded to walk past me like I was nothing.

The need for a glass or ten was riding my back hard. I didn't even know why I was stressing over bitter bitches when I would get the last laugh. I wanted to see how those little bitches were going to feel when their mom died in front of them, and I came and snatched their inheritance. When I turned around, I saw my wife gliding down the steps.

Isis looked like royalty wearing an African print maxi dress in purple, gold, and black. Her hair was braided and wrapped intricately around her head in a crown. Her look was reminiscent of the motherland in all its glory. Resplendent was the word I would use to adequately describe the poise and grace in which her aura shined. You wouldn't have been able to tell that she was sick just an hour ago. When she reached the bottom step, I grabbed her hand and pulled her in my arms.

"What do you say to a man who holds all the world's beauty in his hands daily?" I said and kissed her nose.

"I would tell him always to remember the favors of his Creator and never disgrace it," she said in response and kissed my lips deeply.

I put her hand in mine and led her to the table. Once at her seat, I pulled her chair out and seated her. Across the table, I saw Nefertiti engaged in a conversation with Fahraad, and I almost got jealous. I gave him the best that life had to offer, and he never uttered a word, but he was talking animatedly with the enemy. I heard the door again, and I excused myself to answer the call. I opened the door, and Fahrice stood there.

"Glad you could make it, son," I said to piss him off.

"Cut the shit, where is my brother?"

"He is here, but I need you to press the button and wipe her clean out, when I tell you to."

"Alright, man, anything you say. I want my brother." Just like the pussy he was, he bent to my will.

"Well, come on inside and act as if you love me. Tonight, will be a dinner to remember," I said while letting him in. When we arrived at the dining room table, I announced my guest.

"Everyone, I would like to introduce my son, Fahrice. Fahrice, those are your stepsisters, Nefertiti and Makeda, and this is my lovely wife, Isis." Isis stood up to greet him, but not before I noticed the look that passed between Nefertiti and him. They probably knew each other from some nerd camp.

"Welcome, Fahrice. I'm glad you could join us. It's a pleasure to meet you for the first time, but I hope you won't be a stranger." Isis then enveloped him in a hug, and I wanted to throw up. After tonight, the only people she would meet were the creatures, who consumed her flesh in the grave I'd prepared for her.

"Thank you, ma'am. The pleasure is all mine. I wouldn't miss this night for anything in the world."

Fahrice then went to take the empty seat next to his brother. They embraced for a long moment, and then they started to converse animatedly. I hadn't seen Fahraad that happy since the day before I took him away from his brother.

I took my seat at the head of the table opposite my wife. Shortly after that, the servers start bringing out the food and drinks. When Anajma placed my wife's glass in front of her, I got so excited. I vigorously tore into my beef ribs, baked mac and cheese, and string beans. The dinner chatter was polite at best, and the atmosphere was calm.

My boys and her family are getting along just fine. I felt my phone buzz in my pocket. I read the text and excused myself. I headed to the door and allowed my special guest to enter my home.

With a determined gait, I escorted him to the table and placed him in the seat directly to my left. It went deathly quiet, and I smiled genuinely for the first time in months. Isis looked mad enough to spit fire, and her daughters' eyes mirrored her hatred.

"Fabian, why the fuck is my ex-husband sitting at my dinner table?" Isis accused me vehemently.

"Damn, Isis, is that any way to greet the father of your children?" Pierre asked her with a smirk on his face.

"Pussy, you ain't got no kids. You can call me Mary, issa immaculate conception," Isis spat, and Pierre got mad.

"Still the same bitter bitch you always were."

"To be bitter would imply that I'm upset that I lost something important. Nigga, you are as irrelevant as the tissue I use to wipe my morning shits." Damn, Isis was cutting him to the quick.

"That attitude is the reason why you're in the predicament you are now!" Pierre screamed at Isis.

"What predicament is that? Filthy rich with children who are loved, well-adjusted, and woke? I have a husband who loves the ground I walk on." When she made that last statement, I had to crack up laughing. Pierre joined in and everyone was just looking at us, confused.

"Love the ground you walk on? Bitch, I don't even like the air you breathe." Isis looked like I just slapped the shit out of her mama.

"Pussy, don't come for my mama. You can slide da fuck up out of here," Makeda said to me.

"You little wanna be dyke ass bitch. I will talk to the woman I own, anyway I please, you over-spoiled ass brat. Mind your business and find a dick to suck." That little bitch tried to hop the table, but her twin grabbed her and whispered in her ear. Makeda took her seat, and that was best for her.

Isis stood there, looking at me as if she was trying to hold back her tears. I felt satisfaction down to my nuts at that point.

"Fabian, I don't understand. I thought you loved me. Why are you talking about me as if you hate me?" Isis asked in a small voice, and I loved watching her wilt like a weak bitch.

"The truth of it all is, I do. You are an ungrateful bitch, who thought it was okay to take everything from a man just because he chose up. Because of you, he never got to watch his children grow up. You cut off his money supply when he was the one that upgraded you. For every bitch like you; there is a man like me who comes to get retribution. Fahrice, if you will." Fahrice hesitated as he pulled out his phone and clicked around and pressed a button.

I took a sip of my wine and waited for the second part of this show to jump off. Immediately, I heard her and the girl's phones start going off. I smiled and took another sip of my wine.

"What the fuck did you do? Mommy, all of our accounts are wiped out," Nefertiti said and started clicking buttons just as fast as Fahrice had.

"You can call that reparation. You adding me to your accounts gave me as much authority as you. Back to the bottom from whence you came." Isis jumped up and looked mad enough to chew nails.

"Why the fuck would you ever do this? I have been nothing but good to you. We were supposed…supposed to be…" she said and dropped back in her chair, trying to catch her breath, which looked like it was slowing down. Makeda rushed to her side.

"Were you about to say we were supposed to be a family? I would never join my life with such an undeserving waste of space, such as yourself. In a minute, you will be a distant memory, and all that you have in your empire will be mine. With no contest bang-bang, bitch." I drowned the rest of my glass and watched as the drugs I placed in her wine took effect.

Isis started convulsing, and then her head hit the table. Makeda and Nefertiti were crying as I was sure that her pulse was non-existent. All in a day's work. Pierre looked like he just came in his pants. I knew he was happy with the fifty billion I had transferred to his account. Like a full turkey, I relaxed back in my seat and took it all in. Their sobs were like music to my ears.

"Fahrice, you can take your brother. Your services are no longer needed. Pierre, my man, I hope this was enough and you finally move on with your life. Bitches like her never win," I said before reaching over and giving him dap.

"Thanks, Fabian, this day is the best in my life. I waited years to pay this bitch…" Pierre was cut off by the laughter coming from the end of the table.

I snapped my head around and Makeda and Nefertiti stood next to their mother's chair, dying with laughter. When I look at Isis, her shoulders were shaking, and she stood up. I looked as if I had seen a ghost. I mean, I just watched her die. What the fuck!!! What was happening here?

"Nigga, you should have played with something way safer than me," Isis said to me and it felt like I'd been fucked.

## Chapter 15: Isis

I was looking at the bitch-made nigga, trying to figure out the exact point where he got me fucked up. When I tell you, I laughed so hard at his attempt to kill me. I might have just tinkled on myself. The look on his face when I popped up should have been captured on tape. Now, he and Pierre's bitch asses were looking spooked, as they very well should have been.

"I just watched you die, bitch, how are you alive?" Fabian asked, and that is when I took a seat at the table like the Queen that I was.

"Did you think that a boss like me wouldn't be twelve steps ahead of the game. Your punk ass thought you were going to poison me in my own house, and I wouldn't know about it. Just like you think you've been poisoning me for weeks," I said, and he started looking around, trying to see who snitched on him.

That shit right there was pure entertainment. Then came the moment he accepted that he had been bested.

"Well, it doesn't matter if you are alive. I still crippled your whole empire. I ain't giving you your money back, so now what?" Fabian's arrogant ass had the nerve to say.

"The funniest shit in the world is you thinking you have anything that belongs to me. But I have everything that belongs to you."

When I said that, he snatched his phone out of his pocket, and I watched him press buttons, then his face turned green. Fabian was probably feeling like a two-dollar hoe with no change for a five right now. He loosened his tie as the sweat started pouring down his face.

"Pierre, man, check your account. I don't know what's going on." Pierre took out his phone, and then got wobbly on the legs.

"All my shit is gone. Not one dollar is in any of my accounts. What the fuck, Fabian."

Fabian turned to Fahrice, who was grinning like a Cheshire cat.

"What the fuck did you do, Fahrice? This has never happened before, are you fucking with me?" Fabian was practically foaming at the mouth.

"I didn't do shit, nigga, but my wife might have." Fahrice looked him straight in the eyes and shrugged.

"You don't have a fucking wife. Who is this imaginary bitch?" Fabian barked at Fahrice and

Nefertiti raised her hand and offered him the brightest smile ever.

"That would be me. Hey, father-in-Law," Nefertiti tauntingly said.

"Fahrice, are you kidding me, right now? How did you let your bitch get in my business? So, you're a snake now? My blood is running through your veins and you decide to turn on me."

"First of all, don't address my daughter by anything but her name and don't talk to my son-in-love about loyalty when you don't have a loyal bone in your body. How does a scammer have the audacity to talk to anyone about loyalty and being honest?"

"Bitch, you don't know me."

"Fabian Tahriff Moore, born to Fallon and Tyheim Moore in a small town in Louisiana. Met your first wife in high school and married her before enlisting in the Navy, to which he made it up the ranks to Sargent Major, gave three tours of duty while your wife raised two sons.

"Life for you changed when you came home and found out your wife was a whore to a thug, so, like the bitter bitch you are, you took her children, even the child that does not belong to you. So, with your hurt feelings, you decided to be the proverbial bitch and prey on women and their fortunes. All because his wittle feelings were hurt.

"What disgusts me, even more, is that you blackmailed your son. Made him compromise his morals and clearances to help you lick your wounds. You're the worst type of pussy in this world, and I can't call you a man because your actions show me you wear skirts on the weekends." My read made Fabian turn twelve shades of red and foam at the mouth.

"Who the fuck are you to judge me? All of my actions are justified. You are just like every privileged bitch, who comes from humble beginnings and chooses to be ungrateful like the world belongs to you. This man loved you and gave you a good life. Took care of his daughters and bust his ass to take you from Section 8 living to living at the top. What do you do?

"Take his children then turn them against him. This man has been living life on the bottom since you wiped out all his bank accounts and safes. Then you get mad because he married and moved on after being a thief and decide to fuck with his connect and get him cut off. That is the height of selfishness. How did you ever think you were going to get away with that? Why do you think you get to be selfish with that man's life and get to be happy?" Fabian's bitter ass whined, and it made me hate that I wasted my pussy mileage on his weak ass.

"So, you're telling me that like a hyper side bitch, you decided to take up another man's beef. You just told me that you let Pierre, the ultimate bitch boy, run to you with his problem and like captain save-a-dickhead, you put on your cape to rescue him from little ole me. What in the faggety bullshit are we even discussing?"

"Don't disrespect me like that. You know I'm not sweet, and I'm my own man. I didn't need no help!" Pierre screamed like a little bitch.

"Oh, now you got a voice. You hide behind another man because you couldn't go up against a real one. Well, Fabian, since you are his spokesperson, let me give you a full view of the story and show you why it was safer for you to play in traffic, and why you will pay for the sins of another. Makeda grab my special guests, please."

Makeda excitedly went to the back room of the kitchen. I could tell that Fabian was starting to doubt his stance. But I planned to show these niggas what it meant to go hardbody. Makeda walked back in the room with my guests, and Pierre looked like he wanted to shit his pants.

"Naira, Pierre Jr., what are you doing here?"

"Oh, we here to see Ma hand your ass to you. My name is not Pierre Jr. I could never be the namesake of a coward like you. Call me Phantasm." My baby boy kissed my cheek and Naira grabbed my hand, and I gave it a comforting squeeze. Even with her battered face, she was still beautiful and for that, I would make him pay.

"Take a seat, family. Now that we are all here; Fabian, I will give you the truth, show you your mistake, and judge your actions.

The truth is, Pierre set you up for failure. Pierre has been tucking his tail ever since I beat him at his own game. Sitting before you is the reason why Pierre left, and I never had a choice in his leaving. He was hurt that I birthed him daughters, and he started an affair with Naira that bore him a son. He sent me divorce papers that I signed.

"The day our divorce was finalized, I was moving out as he was parading his new family in front of his old family. I was content to leave and move on with life. That was until he crushed Nefertiti's soul by pushing her on the ground, when she tried to hug him. For every tear my daughter cried; I vowed to make him pay, and I did.

I jumped off the porch and built a team from the muscle. I gave Pierre's team the option to back me or fall with him. Then I took what I felt was necessary to secure my children's brighter future. I even set up an account for his son to have his portion of the empire that I took from the sorry excuse of the daddy, he didn't choose. Phantasm has claimed his inheritance and is now able to take his mother away from the abusive, sorry piece of shit that sits beside you."

When I get done with my spiel, I could see Fabian and Pierre in an intense stare-off. They began exchanging words, but it was all blah-blah-blah because I didn't give a fuck. I didn't have time to waste with their little private conversation.

"Now, let's get to your mistakes. Your first mistake was approaching me. When Nefertiti ghosted Fahrice's computer, she didn't find out much, but it was enough for Makeda--with her perfect little mind--to come up with a plan. I had your picture and no pertinent information. So, when I accidentally bumped into you on purpose in the gym, I was ready for the game.

You never saw me switch our cups at the table, and I was able to get Makeda to run it through CODIS and get the general information, then Nefertiti started to pick your life apart. I read all about your conquests and the women, who lost their livelihoods because of what your ex-wife did to you.

I knew that I had to play it smart, so I allowed you to believe that you were leading me into my demise. Now the game changed when my daughter fell in love with Fahrice. We knew he played a part but just not what. So, when he came to confess, we knew we had an ally.

"The biggest mistake of all was teaming up with a loose lip hoe. My son-son Phantasm had been creeping around Pierre's home, catching all the loudmouth conversations between you two. The first time he heard you was by accident, and he came to tell me immediately, then volunteered to be my spy. So, as you were planning my end, I was setting up yours."

I nod my head and everyone on my side stood up, brandishing their gun of choice. By now, Fabian looked sick to his stomach, and Pierre was damn near in tears. Oh well, such is life.

"Your actions are deplorable and a disgrace to all men in the world. You have pillaged and plundered many lives and tainted many souls. You have failed at fatherhood, marriage, life, and for this, you will pay. For your disloyalty, the attempt on my life, the attempt on my empire, and for all-around having me fucked up, I sentence you to death. All in agreeance, say Aye!!!"

"Aye!!!" everyone chorused together

"Today, I stand before you as your judge, jury, and executioner. May your souls burn slowly in hell and the last thing you remember is that playing pussy, got you fucked." With that, we all raised our guns.

*BLOCKA...BlOCKA...Ratta-Tat-Tat*

## THE END

Other books by Nadine Frye:

Pure Melody

A Savage and His Ridah 1-3

Music of My Life: Melodies, Blues and Hip-Hop

Young Girl Lost: Lyrica's Cry

That North Philly Hood Love Ain't No Fairytale

I Love Him But My Soul Craves Another 1-2

# All About Nadine Frye

Nadine Frye was born and raised in Philadelphia, PA. Coming from the inner-city never stopped her ability to dream big. Being raised in a large family, we used our creative minds to have fun. Making plays and songs and any other things we could dream. In her younger years, you could see her head inside of a book more often than experiencing the outdoors.

In her teen years, a personal tragedy unleashed a world of sadness and hurt only Her notebook could understand. Songs and poems poured from her soul, and for years, it was to feel the relief from her heart. She begins sharing small things with her close circle of friends. It was their motivation and that of her mother and sisters that she shares her talent with the world. That was the beginning of dreaming bigger.

She now resides in Washington, DC, where she wears many hats including Mother and Wife and she graciously adds the hat of an author to her line up.

Personal Quote

"Life is about evolving. Each day is a journey, Each year is a teacher, and every lesson should be applied." -Nadine Frye

Author Page:

https://www.facebook.com/PurpleLyricFandom/

Instagram: @purplelyricfanlife

Twitter: @AuthorNadine

Email: purplelyricfandom@gmail.com

CPSIA information can be obtained
at www.ICGtesting.com
Printed in the USA
LVHW041945061120
670968LV00003B/503